The Victim

by

Jonas Saul

PUBLISHED BY:
Imagine Press Inc.
Ebook ISBN: 978-1-927404-18-8
Paperback ISBN: 978-1-998047-04-8
Hardcover ISBN: 978-1-998047-20-8

The Victim
Copyright © 2012 by Jonas Saul

The Sarah Roberts Series

Dark Visions (One)
The Warning (Two)
The Crypt (Three)
The Hostage (Four)
The Victim (Five)
The Enigma (Six)
The Vigilante (Seven)
The Rogue (Eight)
Killing Sarah (Nine)
The Antagonist (Ten)
The Redeemed (Eleven)
The Haunted (Twelve)
The Unlucky (Thirteen)
The Abandoned (Fourteen)
The Cartel (Fifteen)
Losing Sarah (Sixteen)
The Pact (Seventeen)
The Terror (Eighteen)
The Chase (Nineteen)
The Betrayal (Twenty)
Sarah's Return (Twenty-One)
The Hunt (Twenty-Two)
The Delivery (Twenty-Three)
The Trap (Twenty-Four)
The Ultimatum (Twenty-Five)
The Depraved (Twenty-Six)
The Condemned (Twenty-Seven)
Payback (Twenty-Eight)
The Unknown (Twenty-Nine)
Wrath (Thirty)
The Damned (Thirty-One)
The Game (Thirty-Two)

The Decoy (Thirty-Three)
The Disappearance (Thirty-Four)
The Whole Truth (Thirty-Five)
Alex (Thirty-Six)
Parkman (Thirty-Seven)
Darwin (Thirty-Eight)
Aaron (Thirty-Nine)
Remains To Be Seen (Forty)

The Jake Wood Novels

The Immortal Gene (Book One)
The Immortal Target (Book Two)

Standalone Novels

'Til Death Do Us Part
The Drowning
The Woman in the Woods
The Threat
The Specter
The Mafia Trilogy
A Murder in Time
Frequency of the Dead

Co-Authored Novels

Collision Course (Written with Gary Ponzo)
There Will Be Blood (Written with Rania Stone)
The Soulless (Written with Rania Stone)

Short Story Collections

Twisted Fate (Tales of Horror)

Twists of Fate (Tales of Hope)

Chapter 1

SARAH ROBERTS HATED THIS part of the game. The sitting, the waiting, locked in her underground cell, writing out her dead sister's notes for Hank Frommer, her active role in dealing with the messages all but abolished.

It had been at least six days since Hank had locked her in the underground bunker. Boredom could be defined as staring at the walls, studying the corners and edges in minute detail until she felt she was losing her mind. The food was worse. No one cooked. It was all takeout, and breakfast was last night's takeout.

She had supplied Hank with five days of prophecies written on little pieces of paper. Each morning he had entered her cell, acknowledged what she had said the previous day to be true, and picked up the next one.

It was almost time for Hank's personal prophecy. The one that was supposed to get Sarah out of her prison in North Bay, Ontario's American facility, sixty stories under the earth.

Day one's prophecy had been a car accident where a

pregnant mother needed to be delayed by twenty seconds to miss a red-light runner. Sarah had instructed Hank to block the woman in the parking lot at the grocery store while pretending to talk on his cell. Wait twenty seconds, and then let her go. He would save the life of her unborn child and the mother.

On day two, a school fight would turn nasty at Widdifield High School. A seventeen-year-old student would pull a knife and spend three years in the system. It was unnecessary, as he had coaxed a student to give it to him earlier to diffuse a different altercation. The seventeen-year-old did the right thing and was now being bullied.

Hank was given all the information he needed to fix it.

Days three and four were domestic disputes. In both cases, the women would be beaten and end up in the hospital, one of them in the ICU for a week.

Again, unnecessary.

Day five was the easiest. Hank had taken the note that morning and ran with it. One of his guards was going to have a heart attack and die on shift at 3:17 p.m.

Sarah had no idea what Hank had done with the information she had supplied him. Each morning, her breakfast had arrived. After that, Hank was buzzed into her room and asked for another prophecy.

But all that was over now. The next message was about Hank's wife and how she would die tomorrow in downtown Toronto. Hank believed in Sarah by now and would take her seriously when she finally told him about Joan Frommer's death.

She waited for Hank to enter her cell so she could inform him of the grim news and how he could stop it. All this would be over soon. She had done what he'd asked. She had supplied him with real-time crystal-ball prophecies. That had been the deal. She had complied to get the Sophia Project men off her back for good.

But compliance came with a price, and Sarah wasn't willing to pay anymore. She held the last prophecy in her hand and contemplated ripping it up. She'd done her part. They would work with her now. Release her. Did she really have to tell him that his wife was about to be killed? Or couldn't she? If it was her husband, would she want to know?

Of course, I would.

The door buzzed and opened.

Sarah slipped the note into her pants pocket and crossed her arms.

Hank Frommer stepped inside the small room, followed by two armed guards. He eased the door closed behind him. He looked better than previous days, dressed in a corduroy jacket, beige slacks, and spit-shined shoes.

"What are you dressed up for?" Sarah asked. "We heading somewhere special?"

He regarded her with half a smile. His eyes narrowed as he looked her up and down. A creepy vibe coursed through her. Or maybe he brought the cyanide he'd prepared for her untimely demise, which was why he needed his two guards for muscle.

Just try it, she thought. *The knowledge of your wife would die with me.*

Her hands clenched, feet ready to spring.

"Rod Howley called," Hank said at last.

Sarah uncoiled. "What'd he want?"

Hank hadn't talked to her all week. Nothing about Drake

Bellamy, nothing about her parents, or if anyone was looking for her. She was cut off from society down here. She hadn't seen the sun for a week and had no idea what the hell was happening topside.

The armed men moved closer, flanking her. Hank must've brought them because he had something disturbing to tell her and wanted to know he'd leave the room in one piece. Or they had a plan for her that she wouldn't agree with. There was no good reason for them to be here, any way she looked at it.

"He wanted you," Hank said.

"Me?" Sarah asked, eyebrows raised. "What would he want with little old me?"

"Come on, Sarah." Hank leaned back against the wall by the door and rested on his shoulder blades. "We both know Rod lied to us about you, trying to pass you off as having no abilities. After what you did for me this week, we know that's not true. What we want to know is why he would do that." He raised his index finger and waved it. "You don't know Rod like I do. He's dedicated. A company man. Nothing could sway him. So tell me, what do you have on him?"

Sarah shook her head. "You sicken me."

"How's that?"

"Instead of fighting your kind, I decided to let you in. We have a deal. You see what I can do, and we work together for the good of mankind and yada yada. But instead, I'm locked up for a week in this bunker with no contact with the outside. I'm your little prisoner. Then Rod wants to see what's happening, and you think that's on me. I have no idea why Mr. Howley would lie about my abilities. Maybe he knows you're an asshole. Maybe he knew I would be subjected to this kind of treatment and wanted to spare me from the likes of you. It's not my job to figure it out. I didn't employ Rod. You guys did. You figure it out."

Hank pushed off the wall. "Fair enough. Got any notes for me?"

Sarah glared at him, in no mood to help right now. "No."

She knew she would tell him eventually, but not until she was ready. Especially not when she was angry. She had to take the power back, even if it was a little at a time.

"Really?" he asked. "Not even a little message? No expectant mothers about to have an accident, no kids with knives or guards that need a doctor."

"Did you attend to my notes personally?" Sarah asked.

"Each and every one."

She stepped closer. Both guards moved with her in unison. Hank waved them down.

"How did they turn out?" she asked.

"You were bang on. Not a single person deviated from what you said. To be honest, I'm amazed. You're the best little psychic we've ever had."

"Great. So when do we leave?"

The door to the room buzzed and then opened. Hank stepped over and leaned against it. "We don't leave. When you dry up, and there are no more messages, that's when you leave … in a body bag."

"What?" She hated it when someone felt they could threaten her so easily as if they were talking about the weather.

While Hank leaned on the door, his guards edged even closer. "You didn't think we could ever let someone like you loose on the streets, did you? You have the ability to change the future. We can't have that. We want to study you, get you to foretell future political events."

If she lunged for him, she wouldn't make it. All he had to do was slip out and slam the door. She wouldn't get three steps before the guards were on her.

"What about the five messages I gave you this week?" Sarah asked, her jaw tightening.

"I already told you they came true."

Then she realized what Hank had done as she studied his eyes. He had allowed the prophecies to go … unchecked. The muscles in her face slackened with the realization. Hank was a monster. That he could allow the expectant mother to have her car accident, the boy with the knife, those women in the hospital, and his own guard.

"That's right." He broke into her thoughts. "They all happened as you predicted." He grabbed a few newspapers from outside the door, then turned back to her. "Here, read these. It's the North Bay Nugget. They ran three of the five stories you warned us about." He moved back into the room a couple of feet. "Now, give me another prophecy today, and maybe I'll let you keep breathing. In the meantime, as Rod's employer, I'll go find out why he didn't do his job with you. I'll go 'figure it out,' as you told me to."

Hank's voice grated on Sarah's nerves. She didn't want to hear him anymore. Tears welled in her eyes, and her stomach felt like a bowl of rocks.

How could he let my messages go unchecked? That's not what they were for.

All week, message after message came in. She'd thought he was helping those people, saving them from their own dreadful fate. Instead, he sat on the sidelines and watched the pain and suffering like it was his own macabre show. Her faith in humanity and understanding of it sank to a new low at that moment. Why did she even bother anymore?

"It's okay, Sarah," Hank said. "If those events were supposed to happen to those people at those set times, then who are we to step in and change that? You may be able to see the future, but we aren't God, and we won't pretend to be. Who gave us the right to alter the future? That's the foundation of our organization. We hunt real psychics to quiet them. Eventually, you will die down here, Sarah Roberts, and there's nothing anyone can do about it. Not you, not me, not even God."

Hank laughed loudly as his armed men headed for the door and slipped out. Hank finished laughing abruptly, smiled at her, and waved goodbye like they were old friends.

She moved with speed and agility, making it two steps before Hank could react. Then she was off the ground, diving at him, hands outstretched, aiming for his throat.

Hank disappeared behind the door, slamming it before she reached him. The familiar buzz of the lock engaged as she smacked the back of the door, then hit the floor and rolled to cushion the fall, the breath momentarily knocked out of her.

"We'll see about playing God, Hank," she whispered between breaths. "We'll see who dies down here first, motherfucker."

Chapter 2

SARAH CURLED UP IN the corner of her cell and wrapped her arms around her legs. She wondered why she was here in the first place and how her sister, Vivian, had let it happen. What was the purpose of life when there were people like Hank Frommer? Was it Vivian's fault? Why give Sarah five messages for Hank just to have them come true and secure her in this hellhole? Weren't they supposed to help people?

Sarah understood that there was too much carnage in the world to help everybody, but she could make a difference, even if that difference were small. Every bit counted. That's why she did what she did. When Vivian sent a message through her, she complied. Maybe the people she helped weren't supposed to have bad things happen to them, but by some odd twist of fate, they got stuck in front of the fate train.

In the past, Sarah had helped strangers avoid being kidnapped, tortured, raped, beaten up, and even broke up a human trafficking ring. She had done good deeds and freed numerous people from the shackles of evil, performing random acts of kindness times a million. But all it ever got her was more vileness. Maybe that was the balance. Maybe she had to deal with the filth and scum, so the people she liberated didn't have to. If that was the case, she was okay with it. Over the years, she had grown stronger and better able to deal with it.

But Hank Frommer was a different animal. He was smart and powerful. Most of her adversaries were small-time crooks, running from the law, making mistakes, and afraid of doing the time. Hank worked for the American government on a black project that put massive resources and people at his disposal. Unless Sarah could out-think Hank, she would die at his hands.

She jumped at the door buzzer. Men filed in, one after another until she counted eight. All armed, they stood in a semi-circle with an open door between them.

"What?" Sarah asked. "You don't think you have enough men? A 120-pound girl to eight armed men. Wow, you guys really are pussies."

To their credit, none of them budged at her taunt.

The door opened wider, and Hank stepped in.

"Give it to me," he said.

"Give you what?"

"Don't make me take it by force. I may not be able to control my men. Some of them have urges, working down here night and day."

Sarah smiled. "I have urges, too. I see one cock, and I break it and kill the man who showed it to me. If I'm touched inappropriately, I will break the hand that touched me. Those are my urges. So, let's see whose urges are stronger, shall we?"

"Hold up," Hank said. "We aren't here to see who has bigger balls. We all know what you can do. I was there the night we picked you up, remember? All I want is the note in your pocket."

Sarah checked the corners and upper ceiling. She couldn't see any cameras.

How did he know?

"The cameras are hidden," Hank said. "We've been watching you the whole time."

That meant they'd seen her sleep, bathe and use the toilet.

"You sick bastard."

"Sarah, come on, don't be foolish. There's no way we couldn't watch you. You've been on suicide watch since you came in here."

She pushed her back up the wall to stand. "Why would you have me on suicide watch? I'm not going to kill myself."

"Do you know how many psychics we lose down here after they realize they're never going to the surface or back home? More than half of them do it for us. But you, no, I want you to last a while longer."

"Fuck you, Hank. I mean that. Really, fuck you."

"Poetic. Sweet. Sincere. Now, give me the note, or I will take it."

Four men broke from their rigid positions and moved within a foot of her. Two of the men were sweating as if they were afraid. One of them had a cold stare, and the other looked dead behind his eyes like he'd shut down years before.

Sarah reached for her pocket. A couple of guards

flinched, their hands sliding up their weapons.

"Take it easy," Sarah said. "I'm just getting the note."

She reached into her pocket slowly, so she didn't get shot by a nervous trigger finger. When the paper was in her grasp, she pulled it out and rolled it into the palm of her hand.

"Hank, I have to warn you about this one."

"Just give it to me."

"No, on this one, you need me."

"Yeah, sure, nice try. Hand it over."

"Hank, listen. Remember what you said earlier about not changing the future? About not altering fate? We're not God. Remember you said that? Well, I think you'll need to reconsider."

"Hand it over, or it will be taken from you. You're out of options, Sarah."

"It's about your wife."

That stopped him. It was subtle. His head rose a notch, eyes widened, and his nostrils flared, then it was gone. "Is this a joke? Did you write it, or Vivian?"

"Check the cameras. You saw me write the note. That means you can reference the last five days and see what state I was in when writing the notes that came true. In my automatic writing state, I black out. I can't fake what I don't know how to do."

He extended his palm. "The note."

Sarah handed it to the man closest to her. He walked over to Hank and passed it off without looking at it.

Hank unfolded the paper and scanned the writing. He looked up, his eyes glazed.

"Are you saying this is real?" Hank asked.

Sarah nodded.

"And to fix this, I need to take you with me? Just like it says here?"

She nodded again.

"No," he said. "No, it won't go down like that. Because if something happens to my wife, I will kill you, Sarah Roberts. You will cease to be of use to me." His voice cracked with emotion, but he collected himself fast, afraid or unwilling to show emotion in front of the troops. He backed out of the door, his men following one by one.

A moment later, alone, Sarah realized she had touched the one thing that got inside Hank. He did have the capacity to love. He did love. When it came to his job, like most men, he compartmentalized it. Hurting and killing people was what he was paid to do. At his job, people were something that had to be dealt with. Anywhere else, people were someone. When he was at home, that someone was special, which was entirely different.

Was it enough to get Sarah out of her prison? Would he reconsider taking her along?

Something inside told her he wouldn't and that she would never see the sun again.

Or anyone she loved.

Chapter 3

AN ALARM SOUNDED IN the complex somewhere down the corridor. With no clock in her cell, the only concept of time Sarah had was lights out, which happened every evening. In the mornings, her cell lights would flicker to life. Currently, her cell had been dark for at least most of the night. The alarm resounding throughout the complex startled her awake.

Footsteps pounded down the hall outside her door. Someone shouted. Another alarm, closer, chimed in, adding to the cacophony.

If it was a fire, would they release her or let her burn in her prison?

She stretched to awaken her muscles and got to her feet. After feeling her way to the door in the dark, she waited. She would use the chaos to her advantage and make a break for it if they opened her door.

Someone ran by outside her door. Another man shouted. Her stomach clenched. Every passing second meant they weren't coming for her.

Would Hank let his prized psychic go that easily? Sadly, she realized he probably would. It would save him from having to kill her himself.

The door buzzed. It opened slightly, letting in light from the corridor.

The tip of a gun entered first. Sarah waited. She needed to see the hand, the arm of her visitor, something she could break.

The door slowed and then stopped. Sarah got ready but wasn't prepared for the door slamming inward. It happened so fast that it caught her unawares, banged her arm, and shoved her off balance. She dropped to one knee, spun around, and quickly recovered, returning to her feet.

Two men stood at the open door. Hank and one of his guards. The guard held the gun.

"What's this?" Sarah shouted over the noise of the alarm in the hallway outside the open door. "Gonna use a bullet instead of cyanide? Coward!"

There was enough light to see the look on Hank's face. He was surprised she knew about the cyanide. He tapped the guard on the shoulder and stepped around him.

"Come with us, Sarah," he shouted as he reached out his hand.

"Fuck you," she yelled back.

"Sarah, I need your help. I'll explain on the way. There's a helicopter waiting for us. Now, please, we're running out of time."

He edged closer. She ran through her options. She was dead anyway, whether he was taking her to be killed or not. If he was telling her the truth and there really was a helicopter, this was her best chance at escape.

"Tell dickhead over there to put his gun away, and I'll come peacefully."

"The gun isn't for you," Hank yelled, his hand still extended.

"What?"

"The gun is for anyone who gets in our way. Now, come on."

Hank turned for the door and checked the hall. He looked back at her and gestured for her to follow, then left, not waiting to see if she was coming.

It hit her like a slap in the face. Hank was breaking her out.

Sarah moved. She followed the two men down a couple of corridors and toward an elevator. Hank swiped a card in the reader by the elevator door, and a little light flashed green.

Wet spots had formed under Hank's armpits. He brushed aside the wet hair resting on his brow.

"What happened?" Sarah asked. "The alarms catch you in the shower?"

Hank studied the corridor behind them. His eyes flickered to her and then away again.

"There's a fire in another section. It's hot down that way." He glanced at her and shrugged. "I sweat in heat like any other man."

"A complex like this," Sarah said, waving her arms around, "you'd think they would have safety measures for little fires."

Hank glared at her. "This isn't a little fire."

The elevator pinged.

"You sure we should be taking an elevator during a fire?"

Sarah asked. "Don't they always caution people not to do that?"

The elevator doors opened. Hank and his guard stepped inside.

"C'mon, Sarah. We aren't climbing fifty flights of stairs to the tarmac. The fire is contained in another area of the complex."

Sarah stepped inside the elevator. The door closed behind her, cutting off most of the drilling alarm noise. She leaned back into the wall as the elevator ascended. Dozens of questions raced through her mind, but she kept her mouth shut. Whatever was happening, she was being taken to the surface. The way Hank had been talking, she didn't expect that to ever happen.

The guard looked worried. Other than being wet and looking exhausted, Hank appeared relieved.

"What's really going on here?" Sarah finally asked, not able to help herself any longer. She needed to know what to expect on the surface. It had been a week since they had lowered her into the underground complex. Within minutes, she would be outside again in what she guessed was morning.

"You're going to help me save Joan."

"Why? You changed your mind about not altering the future?"

"No, I haven't."

"You're blubbering."

"I'm what?" Hank asked.

"You're not making sense. Earlier, you said your mandate was to stop people like me. 'We aren't Gods,' you said. What's changed?"

"Nothing's changed."

"Oh, for fuck's sake. You're such an idiot. Do you even know how to talk, how to have a conversation?"

"I'm not going to change the future," Hank said. "You are."

"Me?"

"Yes, you."

"How?"

"You're going to approach my wife, threatening her with harm and make her run away before she's mugged and killed, as your note predicts. That's you changing the future, not me."

"Is that why you set the fire? To find a way to get me out?"

Hank stared at the elevator's panel without responding. She understood. He couldn't admit arson in front of a loyal guard.

The elevator slowed. The guard moved closer to the door and raised his weapon in preparation for what might meet them on the other side.

Hank pulled a pair of sunglasses from his shirt pocket and handed them to Sarah.

"Here, put these on. You haven't seen the sun in almost a week. It might blind you."

Sarah slipped them on.

As the door opened, the rotors of a helicopter revved up. Hank grabbed her arm and led her along a tunnel toward the surface, the guard a few paces ahead.

The helicopter came into view, a pilot at the controls behind the front bubble window. Sarah examined the area, taking it all in. For every second they were on the surface, she was determined to escape Hank's clutches. He would never take her down into the bowels of the complex again. There would be no going back.

The guard ran ahead toward the helicopter, Hank and Sarah following. The fire alarms were silent out here, but the rotors were too loud to talk over.

They hopped in, and Hank shut the door.

"Go, go," he ordered the pilot as he tapped him on the shoulder.

Sarah sat facing Hank and his guard, who still held his weapon.

She grabbed the headset that dangled beside her and placed it over her ears. Seconds later, they lifted off. Sarah glanced out the window and watched the ground move away. The city of North Bay sprawled out toward the lake from the hill where the complex was built.

"Why?" Sarah spoke into the microphone that wrapped around her face from the headphones. "Why all the commotion? Just to break me out?"

Hank adjusted his headset. "I'd never get authorization to let you leave. Not until you're either dead or being transferred to the States for testing."

His voice came through metallic, tinny.

"Testing?" she asked.

He nodded. "We don't meet many like you, Sarah. There's been a few, but they're hard to find. When they're as good as you, the higher-ups like to examine your brain and find out why you can do what you do."

"This little foray into saving Joan—nothing's changed. When we're done, you're taking me back, right?"

He nodded.

She looked out the window to think. The sun hung low, still before noon. They were flying low over a large lake to her right, southbound.

"Let me ask you something."

"Go ahead," Hank said. "Ask anything you want. We're the only ones on this channel. The pilot and my guard here can't hear us."

"How have you managed Drake Bellamy and my parents? You picked me up a week ago from downtown Toronto when I was having dinner with Drake. He would have questions. My parents would want to know what happened to me. What about Parkman? He followed me all the way to Europe. I'm sure he's been asking about me."

While she talked, Hank's smile widened.

"What?" she asked. "What's so funny?"

"You really want to hear about that? You won't like the answer."

Her stomach dropped.

What could he possibly say that would piss me off more?

Hank nudged the guard beside him and motioned with the gun to train it on Sarah. Then he lifted the guard's headphones up and shouted something into his ear. The guard turned in his seat to face Sarah.

"What's that for?" Sarah asked.

Hank met her stare. "I just told him that you're getting angry and might attack us midair. I told him to shoot you in the kneecap if you leave your seat."

"I'm not angry, but I will be if he doesn't point that thing a little to the left or right."

Hank reached over and guided the tip of the weapon so that it aimed a little to her left. It was still facing her general direction but not at her.

"Why would you tell him I'm angry?" Sarah asked.

"Because of what I'm going to tell you."

She waited, not wanting to suppose anymore. Whatever he had to say, she needed to hear it.

The helicopter banked to the left, straightened, and continued forward, the pilot pushing the machine hard.

"As far as the world knows," Hank said, "you're dead."

"What?" Sarah screamed into her mouthpiece.

The guard turned his weapon toward her and held it with both hands. She ignored him.

"Why the fuck is that? What did you do?"

"It's how it works."

"How what works? You better start explaining yourself, or this helicopter doesn't make it to Toronto. I've been shot before. I can kill you with more than one bullet in my body. Start talking."

"You are a victim. Actually, Sarah Roberts, you were the victim on the first day you told us about the accident with the pregnant woman. Since we knew where an accident was going to take place, we added your DNA to the scene and made sure everything was burned beyond recognition." He smiled. "Your DNA was tested at the crash site after the fire that consumed the two vehicles. The newspapers did a huge exposé on you. Editorial columns across North America made you into a hero, covering your exploits from five years ago until the day you died. You went out with international coverage. Can't say that about many of my other exploits."

Her face grew hot, and the inside of her palms moistened. What would her parents be going through? How would Parkman handle it after all they had been through together? She needed to let them know that everything was okay. She needed to let them all know that she was alive.

"I know what you're thinking," Hank said with that stupid smile still plastered to his ugly face. "But it's no use. Your funeral was two days ago. Police officers from around North America attended. You were quite something in your time."

"Why?" was all she could ask as her mind raced with a thousand possibilities.

"Because you are dead, as far as the world is concerned. As I said earlier, you work for the U.S. Government now. After we do this thing in Toronto, you'll be transferred to the States for testing. After six months or so, I have no idea what they do with the subjects, but I can tell you that they never go home."

Rod Howley popped into her head.

"Didn't you say Rod called about me?"

Hank nodded.

The helicopter banked so hard to the left Sarah had to hold onto the seat. It righted, and she adjusted herself. The guard still held his weapon out in front of him, but his arms showed weariness. Hank saw his struggle and motioned with his hands to lower the piece.

"Rod called because he knows the procedure. Which means he knows I'm still alive."

Hank nodded.

"And he wants to keep me alive," Sarah added.

"It appears that way." Hank shook his head in disgust.

She remembered Vivian's note from a week ago, right after she'd arrived at the complex.

"It's Rod, isn't it? He will mug Joan and kill her unless

you take me to Toronto for an exchange."

Hank nodded again. "You're smart. He's already got her. We're supposed to exchange you in the Allandale Centre food court."

"But you're intent on not letting me go or letting Rod live, are you?"

Hank clapped his hands a few times, signaling she got it right. With the sound of the rotors and the headphones, his hand clapping went unheard.

With Sarah officially dead to the world, Hank could do whatever he wanted to her, and no one would ever know.

Even if she called for help, Dolan, Esmerelda, or Drake would think it a cruel joke that someone would call and pretend to be Sarah, no matter how similar she sounded.

She really was a victim. Every time she turned around, someone was trying to kill her. Or, in this case, already had. Whether it was the bad guys or the good guys—supposed good guys—she had to fight. This was no different.

She forced her emotions down. She wouldn't cry in front of Hank. When she thought of her parents' pain, she became overcome with grief. Her parents were strong. They could handle it until she resurfaced. Parkman would smile with a toothpick in his mouth when he saw her again and mutter how he knew she wasn't dead all along.

All she had to do was get away from Hank.

And to do that, she had to kill him.

Chapter 4

THE HELICOPTER LANDED JUST after lunch. She learned that it was Saturday and the Allandale Centre on Yonge Street in downtown Toronto would be swarmed with shoppers. Rod had chosen a high-traffic area for the exchange. Also, according to Hank, doors leading to the underground subway were merely twenty feet from the last food court table.

But he explained how he had covered it all in advance. Six men waited for Rod to show himself. Two were inside a sporting goods store, two were eating KFC at a table, and two were walking around the area. They would cruise up and down the aisles one floor above the food court section of the mall, as it was open and exposed to upper levels.

Sarah had saved Rod's life after he had been shot in the basement of a madman's cage. She surmised he was attempting to return the favor. What concerned her was Vivian's silence. It would help if her sister could give her a little inside information, something to lead her and set her in the right direction. But Sarah hadn't been alone or with a pen and paper so Vivian could step in and advise.

You could've said something yesterday, Vivian.

But then she remembered that Hank would've read the note because they'd been watching her the whole time.

They led Sarah from the helicopter to a waiting four-door sedan. Hank sat beside her in the car, and then it was underway.

"What's in it for me?" Sarah asked.

"Nothing, really."

"Then why am I here?"

"Because we had to bring you for proof of life."

Sarah turned and looked at him. "Are you saying I'm walking into a trap? Once the exchange takes place, and I'm with Rod, will you kill us both? Is that it?"

Hank pulled out a handkerchief and dabbed at his forehead and face. He stashed it back in his pocket and met her gaze.

"Sarah, look, you've been a real sport. You came with me willingly when we approached you at the restaurant in Toronto last week." He stopped and chuckled. "Well, almost willingly. Anyway, you supplied me with five prophecies, and now the most important one. I appreciate that. But now I need your help to save my wife. I know Rod, and he won't have a problem killing Joan. I've worked with him for years. He was one of the best agents we've ever had."

"So what are you saying? I'm free to go if I help you?" Somehow she didn't think so.

"What I'm saying is I'll give you a chance."

"What kind of chance?" Sarah asked.

"I'm willing to hand you off to Rod. Once my wife is in my grasp, my men have orders to kill you and Rod. That'll give you at least ten seconds to get away."

She gaped at him. "You're kidding, right?"

He shook his head.

"That's not a chance, that's a death sentence. You're giving me enough time to walk over and stand against the wall for the firing squad."

"I'm sorry you feel that way because you can do a lot with ten seconds."

"You're insane. Can you even hear yourself?" She collected her breath, closed her eyes for a second, and asked, "And what if I refuse?"

"Sarah, I know your talents. Even you can figure it out."

What was Hank talking about? How could ten seconds in a crowded mall give her any kind of chance? She looked down at her hands. They weren't cuffed. Her ankles had no restraints.

"You're offering me ten seconds to run? Is that it?"

"Yes."

"That's not a lot of time. In fact, it's nothing."

"In an open field, you'd be right. In a crowded mall, that's a lifetime. I'm not so above the law that I can order my men to shoot indiscriminately. There can be no, to minimal collateral damage. The mall will be filled with women and children. You get ten seconds. Then we come after you. That's the deal. In this case, there's no take it or leave it. If you attempt to escape before the exchange with Rod, my men have orders to execute you with extreme prejudice. There'll be no ten seconds. So, you see, the ten seconds sounds appealing now."

Outside, downtown Toronto raced by the windows. Torontonians walked the streets, going for lunch, shopping, and thinking about the evening barbecue or movie they'd attend. Sometimes she yearned for that life. A simpler life.

The car slowed, bringing her back to the here and now.

"Joan's life hangs in the balance," Hank said. "If you try to run, we both know you won't get far before my guard shoots you down. I didn't bring him along for his good looks. He's my best shooter. So, I'm asking you to come with me to the food court, present yourself to Rod and then walk to him. Count off ten seconds after Joan is safe with me, and that's my gift to you. That's all I can offer in my capacity. Are we good?"

The car stopped beside the mall doors. The driver turned on the four-ways.

"We good?" Hank asked again.

There was nothing else she could do. For the time being, he had her. Ten seconds was better than one or two if she ran at any other time. But could she trust him to give her that ten-second window when the time came?

Two men stepped up to the vehicle and flanked each side of her door, waiting for it to open.

"We're good," Sarah said. Without meeting his gaze, she muttered, "But you'd better give me all ten of those seconds, or I'll come for you." She stared at him. "Sarah Roberts always gets her man."

Hank laughed. "If I don't give you ten seconds, Sarah, you'll be dead."

"I guess we'll have to see about that."

She opened the door and got out, the men closely flanking. She was a flight risk. Any move now would be met with swift action. She really had no play until she saw Rod.

Hank led the way into the mall, followed by Sarah, her

new escorts, and the guard behind them, his gun now secreted in his waistband.

They entered through double doors by a large McDonald's and started for an escalator to take them down one level. Sarah removed the sunglasses Hank had given her and examined the mall, taking it all in and watching for easy points to exit. Running through all these people with men chasing or even shooting at her didn't look promising. She had to come up with something else. Her odds didn't feel so good.

Hank hadn't tied her hair up. It flowed past her shoulders, needing a trim, similar to what she looked like before going into the complex a week ago. She wondered if anyone would recognize her but dismissed that idea as futile because everyone thought she was dead.

Hank probably left my hair alone so Rod would know me on the spot.

Halfway down the escalator, she saw the doors to the underground subway. From her vantage point, she couldn't see past them. People milled around everywhere, the mall so busy at this early afternoon hour on a Saturday.

Even though she had to figure out a way to escape with her life, she worried about the people eating lunch and shopping in nearby stores. Unbeknownst to them, a shootout was about to take place.

At the bottom of the escalator, Hank motioned for her to come with him. He moved to a large round pillar off to the side and placed her back to it, with him in front of her, a man on either side.

Hank touched his earpiece and mumbled into his lapel. She hadn't noticed his communications setup earlier. She followed his gaze and counted the men he nodded to throughout the food court and above. At a count of eight, her stomach dropped.

Hank had said there were only six. He nodded at another man. Then another.

She grabbed his arm and spun him around. The man on her right wrenched on her shoulder to pull her back to the pillar.

"You said you only had six men," Sarah said. "I count at least nine so far. What the fuck?"

"Calm down," Hank whispered. "I do only have six." He looked left and right to make sure no one was watching them. He nodded at the guard on Sarah's right, and the hand on her shoulder lifted off. "There are at least twenty men in the area waiting for Rod Howley. Local law enforcement was called in. They are working in conjunction with us to stop Rod."

"Geez, when one of your members goes rogue, you guys really show him a good time."

"What Rod has done and what he knows about us—well, let's just say, he can't be trusted. My six men answer to me. The rest of the people assembled here today have no idea who you are or why you're here. They aren't a threat to you. Don't worry, you will still get your timeframe of ten seconds. Rod doesn't get any."

Hank turned away and whispered into his lapel again.

There had been something in his eyes, a flicker, a twitch. She was sure he was lying about something, but she had no idea what. She wondered if the local law enforcement really knew who she was and were no threat to her. Would Hank have given that information up so easily? She knew these Sophia Project men, and their reputation was subterfuge only.

Hank would never tell the locals who she was. He would lie to serve his purpose.

"What have you told the local authorities about me?" she asked.

He spoke into his mic, ignoring her.

Sarah scanned the area. Nothing was familiar. Average Canadian families walked around with shopping bags and babies in their arms, some pushing strollers with no idea what was about to happen at any moment.

Across the labyrinth of tables and chairs, two men with white-powdered faces, wearing long black overcoats, stared at her. She stared back, trying to see if they were watching Hank and his men or her. When she was sure they were watching her, she looked left toward the sporting goods store to see if others were watching her. A quick look to the right toward the rest of the small fast-food restaurants revealed nothing.

When she looked for the two men in black overcoats, they were gone. Something about them disturbed her. She frantically searched the immediate area but didn't see them.

Her hand numbed.

Oh, no, not now, Vivian. I have nothing to write on.

The numbness faded, pins and needles came and went. She flexed her hand and tried to calm her nerves.

I know you're with me. Thanks, Vivian.

"Hank?" she called.

He checked the time on his watch and then half-turned to her. "What?"

"Are any of your men dressed in black overcoats?"

He frowned, met the eyes of his guards, and then brought his attention back to her. "No. Why do you ask?"

"Nothing."

The two men weren't just curious. The look in their eyes held intent. She'd seen it before. They were up to something and weren't part of Hank's crew.

Who are they? Rod Howley's men?

She hopped from one foot to the other. She would only get one chance at this. Her heart rate increased, and adrenaline flowed. She flexed her arms and fingers and waited for Rod to show.

"Hank?" Sarah said again.

"What?" he said without turning around, an edge of agitation in his voice.

"What if Rod calls at the last minute and sets a new place to meet? Or what if he doesn't show at all?"

"He'll show. I'm not worried about that. I know him."

"Yeah, but he'll know you have the place surrounded. Why would he willingly walk into the trap?"

"Because he thinks he holds all the cards. We won't move on him as long as he has Joan, and once he gets you, he thinks we won't move in on him."

"Why's that?"

Hank half-turned to her again. "Because he knows how good you are and doesn't imagine we would kill you. Yet. That's where he's wrong."

"Gee, thanks. Why am I helping you again?"

"You're not helping. You're here because you have no other choice."

"I could kill you with my bare hands within three to five seconds. So I actually do think I have a choice."

"What did you just say?" a voice to her left asked.

She looked into the eyes of a tall, dark-skinned man with

a barrel chest. He towered over her by at least a foot.

"Don't worry about her, Detective Waller. She's here to help the exchange take place."

He scowled down at Sarah. "It sounded like she just uttered a death threat." His deep voice resonated through her. It was the kind of voice she envisioned her husband having one day. The kind that made her feel safe, protected, and cherished.

"She did," Hank said. "She's pissed off that she has to be here, but don't worry about that. She's my problem. Is everyone in place?"

Detective Waller's piercing green eyes turned and met Hank's gaze. "Yes, all my men have been told about your sex offender."

Sarah coughed out a chuckle, then clamped a hand over her mouth.

Detective Waller turned to her and leaned in close to her. "Do you find something funny, little girl?"

Hank reached around and pulled Waller back up by his arm. "As I said a moment before, disregard her. She doesn't understand the gravity of the situation."

"Remind me why she's here again. If this guy is meeting us here, why do you need her? We'll just pick him up. Quick and clean."

"Do you know Parkman?" Sarah asked Waller. "He must be here. How about it? Is Parkman around?"

"I appreciate your cooperation," Hank said to Waller, completely ignoring Sarah. "But I've worked with this guy Rod for many years. He's a professional. The odds of just picking him up quickly and clean are low. We have to do this right, and for that, we need her. Now, are your men in place?"

Waller nodded. He kept sneaking glances at Sarah but didn't say anything more to her. She wondered if he recognized her from all the recent media attention she had gotten.

"Good," Hank said. "It's three minutes to one, so get everybody ready. Howley is probably already here."

Detective Waller took one more look at Sarah and stepped away, disappearing in the throng of shoppers seconds later.

Hank backed into the shadows, crowding Sarah. He lifted his lapel and said, "Everyone, be ready. This is it. First one to spot Howley, radio it in. And remember, he may have his own people with him. No weapons. I repeat, no weapons in the mall. Tasers only. Subdue and secure. Clear?"

Numerous men chimed in, but Sarah could only hear a metallic reply from Hank's earphones.

Her hand went numb again. She shook it off and mumbled, "Not now."

The guards on either side looked at her. Hank half-turned. "What not now?" he asked.

"Nothing." She widened her eyes, smiled, and shrugged briefly like a crazy person.

"What not now?" Hank asked again.

"Vivian is trying to tell me something. I don't like this. Something's wrong here. It doesn't feel right."

Hank scanned the crowd and adjusted his earpiece. "What doesn't feel right?" he asked.

"I don't know. It just … feels off somehow."

"We have a minute left. This is no time for conscience or nerves."

"I'm not talking about nerves, asshole. Rod wouldn't do

this. He wouldn't kidnap Joan and then set up a meeting to exchange for me. He knows you and what you would do to him. Something's not right. The more I think about it, the more it just feels off."

"You know, you're right. This doesn't feel like Rod. But desperate people do desperate things."

"Yeah, so why exchange for me? What does he want with me?"

"You saved his life, didn't you?"

"So?"

"He's returning the favor."

Sarah shook her head. "No, he would do something else. He would contact your superiors or get his own team together to come after me. Hell, he could've organized a visit to your compound and broke me out if he wanted to. But kidnapping your wife? Doesn't feel right. Too personal."

"You're telling me this now because ..." Hank scanned the area again and checked his watch. "This is it. It's one p.m."

"It all happened so fast. The alarm at the complex, you put me on the helicopter. I haven't really thought about it until now."

"Well, it doesn't matter. He's going to show any second. We're out of time."

Chapter 5

Since Sarah woke to sirens in her cell that morning, she hadn't fully grasped the seriousness of the situation. A week in one room, solitary confinement with only a book, her pen, and a pad of paper to keep her company had dulled her senses.

Her food had arrived through a slot in the door. Nothing had tasted good. Hank and his men had been her only visitors. He came each morning and relieved her of any written prophecies from her sister.

They had given her one novel. *Swan Song* by Robert McCammon. She thought of Swan, the main character in that novel now. Even after a nuclear war, Swan carried on and brought life to all she touched. Lucifer had walked the earth, but Swan was untouchable. Evil may have won, but it would never conquer.

Sarah felt like that now. She would walk away from this as long as she was smart. These men had orders to kill her. There had to be an escape without harming the public.

The sporting goods store was no more than twenty feet away. She could cover that distance in seconds. All she had to do was wait for Rod Howley to show up with Hank's wife, and she would be ready. There was no way Hank would order her shot down in the middle of the food court. He was counting on her running out the subway doors or up the escalator to the ground level. That gave him time to chase her and catch her away from all these people. He didn't count on her staying on this level and fighting back. She had nothing but her hands to fight with. They had weapons.

But Rod hadn't shown, and Hank was growing increasingly agitated. He whispered into his lapel and wiped his forehead. His men moved closer, edging around the perimeter of the food court, jockeying for a better position to watch for Howley.

Still, nothing happened.

"Shit," Hank exclaimed, slapping a fist into his open palm. "Where the fuck is he?"

He stepped out farther. Anyone on the level above could see him now.

Sarah waited and watched. This was her only chance. Even if Rod didn't show, she would have to make a break for it. If she was locked in a cell, there was no way Hank would ever let her back out again.

Her hand numbed and then cleared.

I know, Vivian. I'm ready.

Sarah saw her first. A lone woman was standing on the other side of the food court. She looked sickly pale. Her lipstick smeared past her lips on each side of her face making a line across her cheeks. She was crying.

Then Hank saw her.

"Joan?" he whispered. Then louder, "Joan."

He stepped out of position and started across to her. The two men flanking Sarah each grabbed an arm and guided her across the food court behind Hank.

The pale look on Joan's face was a white powder, and the red smears weren't lipstick at all.

It was blood.

Sarah's stomach turned at the sight.

Everyone was on edge now. The guards let Sarah's arms go so they could be ready, one hand on their weapons. A commotion started behind her while Detective Waller's men began the daunting task of cordoning off the area for the safety of shoppers.

Hank reached Joan and asked again and again what had happened. Joan appeared dazed as if she was on drugs. He grabbed her shoulders and shook her.

Sarah watched for her chance.

"What happened?" Hank asked. "Where's Rod Howley? What did he do to you?"

Joan opened her clenched palm and handed Hank a picture. Hank snatched it and studied it. People ran by them, headed for the underground subway.

Sarah had to make a break for it. She had to go now. Any moment, Hank would pay attention to her again, and her chances of escape would decrease quickly.

Another second ticked by as she waited for more chaos. A woman screamed, and a man shouted. She was tempted to turn around to see what was happening but waited. Any second now. Patience.

Hank held the picture up in the air. Sarah caught a glimpse of it.

Run screamed in her head when she saw the image. Hank's face was a mask of surprise and terror.

"Who did this?" he asked.

Joan was crying hard now. She stumbled on her feet.

"What happened to your face, honey?" Hank asked.

Then Joan lost her balance, and Hank stepped forward to catch her. More women screamed. The guards beside Sarah stepped forward to help Hank.

Sarah spun around and locked in on the sporting goods store.

At least three of Hank's men were lying on the mall's tiled floor, white foam seeping from their mouths, writhing on the floor as if in an epileptic seizure. Then they stopped moving, their eyes open, dead.

Another man fell, writhing on the tile floor, arms flailing like a dying cockroach. Then another dropped.

Detective Waller stood by the base of the escalator. He pulled out his weapon and aimed it at the roof.

"Everyone, please calm down," he shouted. "This is a police emergency. Move away from the area."

On the level above, someone screamed. Sarah looked up as a Toronto cop fell to his knees, sputtering white foam.

What the fuck is happening? What's killing everybody?

She held her breath in case it was an airborne agent. Then she breathed out because whatever it was, it seemed to only be going after the cops. Locked, rooted to her feet, her mind reeled. Nothing made sense. She couldn't see the adversary. No one could. Yet Hank's and Waller's men were falling like they were being stung by a killer bee that caused a seizure and death within seconds.

Her hand twitched like Vivian had something to say.

Sarah took that as her reminder to run and stay alert.

Hank held his wife's head in his lap, moving his hand through her hair, tears falling onto her powder-white cheeks. The two guards had stepped away, their guns up and ready.

White powder.

Sarah remembered seeing the two men watching them from across the food court. Their faces were unusually white. They had dressed in long black overcoats. She lowered to one knee and spun in a full circle, searching for anyone with a white-powdered face.

Now knowing what to look for, she located at least three of them, moving around and through the throng of onlookers.

Another man fell. Another woman screamed. A father grabbed his child and ran past Detective Waller. A woman with a stroller almost tripped over a dead cop by her table. A couple of teenagers had been sitting in the center of the melee with heaping plates of Chinese food, their iPhones held high as they recorded the action. Two policemen stepped close and shouted for them to run. They did.

More policemen fell. Sarah was paralyzed, not knowing which way to run, which way was safe.

Hank lay sprawled out beside his dead wife, shaking, foam bubbling from the corner of his mouth.

That was all the prodding she needed.

Sarah hunched over and bolted for the sporting goods store.

As she neared it, the sporting goods store window shattered beside her with a deafening shatter. Sarah dropped to the floor under the glass shower and slid on her stomach as if trying to steal second base. She scrambled on hands and knees out of the range of the fallen shards of the display window until she was around the corner and then slipped inside the store. Behind a rack of hockey jerseys, she chanced a look back into the mall. Pandemonium.

People ran every which way, scattering and screaming as more men fell and twitched a death dance on the tiled floor. Powder-faced men walked among the shoppers and the dead as if their own shopping had ended.

Sweat pouring into her eyes, adrenaline spiking, Sarah watched, transfixed by the horror. The only man she recognized still standing was Detective Waller. She was sure he was the one who had fired at her. He'd barricaded himself inside the booth of a yogurt drink shop, his gun aimed at anyone who ventured too close.

Her arm twitched again. She had to get as far away from the carnage as she could. They had been waiting for Rod Howley to show, but the only sign of Rod was the picture Joan had carried in. Unless the image was altered, it showed a clearly dead Rod Howley. It had happened since the last phone call he'd made to Hank about today's meeting. Rod's face had been covered in white powder, eyes open in a death stare, and white foam mixed with blood dried on his cheek.

Then why set the meeting up? Who was behind it all, and why go after Rod and Hank? Killing members of a black government operation was one thing—she was sure they had enemies—but killing Toronto police officers and local detectives would bring a lot of heat on whoever was behind this massacre.

One of the men in the long overcoats stepped up to the broken window of the sporting goods store and stared through the open space. His eyes stopped on Sarah. He was ugly, his forehead protruding unnaturally. His eyes were a piercing blue, like the eyes of a Siberian husky. He smiled, revealing bottom teeth that were tented, like small pegs, pointy. She shuddered at the image.

He beckoned with the wave of his hand. "Come," he called out.

A policeman stepped beside him and held a gun to the man's temple.

"On the ground," the cop ordered.

The man slowly turned to face the cop, never losing his grotesque smile. He raised his hands slowly. Sarah caught the hesitation of his right hand as it passed the cop's arm. He held something long and silver that resembled the tip of a syringe. Then the white-faced man's hands were high above his head.

Sarah could've counted the five seconds before the cop fell out of her sight line. The man turned back to Sarah and beckoned again.

"Come."

Sarah edged out and stood up on wobbly legs. She hadn't seen this kind of violence and death in some time and wasn't prepared for its sudden impact on her psyche. She asked herself if anyone could ever prepare for what had just happened.

The cop foamed at the mouth, thrashing in his final death throes.

Whatever the men in the overcoats had, it was silent and lethal and killed within seconds.

"Last chance," the man said, his hand still outstretched. "Come."

Sarah stepped back. He had to be wearing a mask of some kind. Padding over his forehead and nasty dentures.

She took another step backward. It was like Dracula was alive and well, asking for her hand in marriage. In any other circumstances, she would've laughed him off.

He shook his head animatedly as she stepped away, his chin almost touching each shoulder. She bumped into something and spun around in a crouch. Another man in an overcoat stood over her.

This is ridiculous.

The man reached out, trying to touch her with whatever was in his hand. She jumped away and bumped into a clothing rack. A female store employee screamed from behind the counter. The man lunged for Sarah. She dropped to her knees and dove under the rack, coming up on the other side.

He was fast, running around the rack, but it gave her enough of a head start to scramble down the aisle toward the back. She knocked over small displays to delay her pursuer. Out of the corner of her eye, she saw him easily hop over the rack of sweat socks.

She ran past the tennis rackets, balls, and badminton section. Then a quick jump over a discount golf ball section and she saw the baseball department in the back corner on the right. She headed for that, whipped a circular rack of sports bras into the aisle behind her, and made it to the baseball bats before the overcoat man could catch up.

She grabbed a Louisville Slugger and, without slowing down, spun on her heels, swinging the bat full circle. It connected with her pursuer's jaw with a crunch. The man dropped like a sack of lead, his hands clutching his ruined mouth, moaning instead of screaming.

Another man with a white-powdered face stepped in

beside her before she could raise the bat again. He jabbed a hand toward her arm, but she jerked out of range and brought her left hand up to ward off the attack, dropping the baseball bat in the same movement. She shoved hard, jamming his hand into his neck. Sarah held his arm there, pushing him away from her, screaming in anger. With her right hand, palm open, she rammed his hand deeper into his neck. His eyes widened as a small yelp escaped his lips.

She let go of him as he fell backward over a display of baseball gloves. He looked at her in panic, brushing at his neck. A small dot of blood formed below his jaw, and then his arms locked, followed by his legs. A moment later, he convulsed, white foam gurgling out of his mouth. She waited for at least seven seconds, watching the man die.

A gunshot rang out in the food court. Women screamed, and a man, probably Detective Waller, shouted for everyone to calm down.

The lights in the sporting goods store went out. Emergency lighting came on.

That broke her stupor.

Sarah ran for the back and exited through the hallways behind the store that led to the garbage compactor the retailers used.

When she reached the street level, she turned up Yonge Street, put the sunglasses that Hank had given her back on, and blended in with the street traffic as sirens shattered the mid-afternoon calm.

Chapter 6

Simon Peter finished wiping the rice powder paste off his face with a wet nap and threw it in the trash can. He stared at his reflection in the dirty bathroom mirror, wondering how it had all gone wrong. How could they have missed their golden opportunity? Sarah had been right there, guarded by police officers. The area had fallen to chaos. His mission had gone as planned until Sarah ran. He hadn't expected that.

His brother Matthew hadn't told him to watch for her to run, but Simon should've been prepared for that. The information had been specific. Get to Sarah Roberts through Rod Howley. Once the meeting had been set, send Rod home. He had served his purpose.

But now Sarah was on the run. Mistakes had been made. They would have to regroup. He needed more information from his brother.

Simon pulled off his hairpiece and wiped his bald pate clean of any glue. He stuffed the hairpiece into a side pocket, adjusted his coat, and lowered his head to whisper a silent prayer. Then he took his sky blue contact lenses out and gently placed them in their container.

A moment later, he checked his remaining two syringes to be certain they were intact and exited the bathroom of the Royal York Hotel.

On the street, he stepped out to a line of taxis. The first one in line was a silver minivan. He hopped in and gave the driver the Dundas/Dixie corner in Mississauga as his destination.

In mid-afternoon traffic, he arrived forty-five minutes later. The driver had attempted small talk and even asked if Simon had heard about the shooting at the Allandale Centre. But Simon remained silent, watching the traffic outside the cab's windows. He had a lot on his mind. How they had missed Sarah when they were standing right beside her was a sin. He had failed God. He wouldn't fail Him again.

He got out in the parking lot of a coffee shop, paid his fare, and slammed the door. The driver squealed away, evidently upset that his passenger hadn't been more talkative.

Simon walked north on Dixie Road. Their prearranged meeting place was still over five blocks away at Dundas and Bloor in an apartment building. All surviving members of the Rapturites were to meet at apartment 1115 when Sarah's rapture was completed, and Simon Peter, their leader, intended to be there on time.

In the Bible, of Jesus' twelve apostles, Simon Peter actively brought people to Jesus, a mission this Simon took seriously. He was the chosen one. He had changed his name legally and took on the role of head of the Rapturites three months ago. The movement was going in the right direction faster than he could have expected. His identical twin brother, Matthew, was quite happy with him.

Getting access to the muscle relaxant, pancuronium bromide, better known as pavulon, had proven easy through one of his new members. This pharmaceutical employee handled the ordering for a giant company in southern Ontario. One hundred milligrams of the fast-acting muscle relaxant would paralyze the muscles in the human body, even the heart muscle, within seven to ten seconds. It was part of the mix they used on death row inmates during executions.

Simon had concocted his own variant but knew, eventually, the experts would be onto what they were using. But they would never be able to track it back to the Rapturites in time. Simon had ordered enough of the deadly toxin to last him a month. Over three hundred syringes with 100 mg of his toxic mix were stored at a secret location that only he knew about. That meant Simon and his faithful apostles could send hundreds of people home to the Lord, as this was the end times, and the Rapture was upon them. It was a mission ordained by the Lord. It gave him great joy to send his fellow man and woman home.

He turned left onto Dundas, his coat flapping in the wind. When he arrived, and the Rapturites met, he would persuade them to regroup and re-attack. Matthew would offer the information needed, and they would help Sarah Roberts get home. She was a good person. They needed her up above. As the chosen one, it was Simon's job to send home the people who were dictated to him. His followers were ready. They were armed with righteous knowledge and the protection of the Lord, yet something went wrong, and he couldn't figure it out.

Mr. Howley had been easy. Rod made the calls to the

man holding Sarah as requested. They held onto Joan Frommer for several days to authenticate Rod's claims. Otherwise, according to Simon's brother, they wouldn't be able to get to Sarah. It had even been Matthew's idea to inject Joan with a slightly diluted mix so she would take a few minutes to succumb, thereby giving her a chance to see her husband before she died.

Simon went over the plans in his head. Everything Matthew instructed had been done. Praise the Lord. But Sarah had gotten away.

Next time, they would be more prepared. Next time, they would swoop down like angels, all of them landing on her at the same time. It didn't matter whether she had multiple injections. Their purpose was divine, their goal heavenly.

Sarah Roberts only had days left to live, and Simon Peter planned on helping her to leave this place, or he would die trying.

Chapter 7

SARAH WALKED NORTH ON Yonge Street, mixing with the crowds on the sidewalk. She kept herself together until she was far enough away that the sirens faded. She made a quick turn onto Wellesley Street and another into an alley beside a city parking lot, where she found relative privacy.

She sat on a wooden bench, brought her knees up to her chest, and wrapped her arms around herself. She had to get it together for the next step. Who were those men with white faces? What did they want, and how could they kill so many people so easily, so quickly? All those police officers …

She shuddered. With all she had been through in her short twenty-five years, she had grown accustomed to seeing people die, but not that many in such a public venue. She had an issue with cops, even hated them at times, but not enough to wish this on them.

Dolan. She had to contact Dolan. Maybe Esmerelda. They could help and offer insight. She would try them before going to her parents because they would be overwhelmed with grief after attending her funeral. It would take them too long to come around and start being productive in any way.

If Dolan and Esmerelda couldn't help, the least they could do would offer shelter until she could locate Parkman. He would help her no matter what. Being a cop, Parkman could possibly pull security footage from the mall or contact the Toronto police and find out who the attackers were.

Hank Frommer had died in the mall. She'd seen it with her own eyes. Rod Howley was dead. Was there anyone left in the Sophia Project to come after her? Could that chapter in her life finally be over?

A beat-up Mazda pulled into a spot six feet away. The driver watched her too long. She wiped her face and nose, got off the bench, and walked the other way.

Hank hadn't given her any money. She still wore the clothes from a week ago when she went to dinner with Drake. She hadn't eaten since yesterday, and the adrenaline had weakened her.

She had to call Dolan. She needed food. Otherwise, she thought she would collapse. And she needed a coffee, hardcore.

She walked back to Yonge Street among the hundreds of people. Her shirt hadn't been laundered in over a week. Sliding on the mall floor had left streaks of dirt. She shook out her hair, layered it over the side of her face, and sat down against the wall of the Scotia Bank at Yonge and Wellesley.

After a moment, she rested her hand on her knee, palm up, head down, and waited. Her hand shook uncontrollably. It added to the overall effect of begging.

It didn't take long. A man in a suit walked by and dropped a dollar coin into her hand. Then a young couple placed two quarters there. When they were out of sight, she shoved all the money in her pocket except for a quarter, which she set on the concrete in front of her. Then she waited for more.

In twenty minutes of resting on the pavement in front of the bank, Sarah accrued seven dollars. She collected the coins, slipped them into her pocket, and walked across the street to the Starbucks, where she bought a tall dark roast and a banana bread. Then she located a pay phone by the parking lot where she had rested earlier.

She downed the banana bread in three bites before she dialed Dolan's number from memory.

After accepting the charges, Dolan's familiar voice said, "Hello?"

"It's so good to hear your voice," Sarah said.

"Who is this … wait, Sarah?"

He sounded incredulous.

"The one and only," she said.

"You're alive!"

She pulled the phone away from her ear. "As far as I know. Hey, you're supposed to be psychic. How come you didn't know?"

"A million questions are running through my head," he said, ignoring her question. "What happened? You died in a car accident. I was at your funeral. It was horrible. We thought we had lost you."

"Let me guess, closed casket, right?"

"Yeah."

She kept an eye on the other side of the street. The last thing she needed was for more white-faced assassins to come up behind her.

"It was all a ruse," she said. "The American government, my own people, snatched me in Toronto a week ago. They flew me up to some compound in North Bay. I got out today."

"Sarah, that doesn't add up. Why would they bury you and then just let you go a week later?"

"They didn't plan on letting me out."

"Oh …"

"It's a long story. I need help. I have no ID, no money, and nowhere to go." She sipped her coffee. It tasted heavenly after a week with only water. "Is Drake still in Toronto? Parkman? I need someone to bring me in and help me get home. I think it's better to see my parents and tell them what happened face-to-face instead of telling them over the phone."

"Yeah, yeah, I understand. Look, I'll make some calls." He paused. "I heard you sip something. You got a drink without money?"

"I panhandled for the money."

He didn't say anything for another moment.

"Sarah, Sarah, Sarah …"

"What?" She could see him shaking his head.

"Nothing. Are you in danger right now?" Dolan asked.

She scanned the street in both directions.

"Probably, but I'm not sure."

"Okay, look, I'll call and book a room for you in a hotel. Put dinner and other expenses you need on the room. My card will cover it. In the meantime, I'll get Drake, Parkman, or someone familiar to meet you."

"Sounds good."

She told him where she was, and after searching the

internet, Dolan suggested she stay at the Courtyard by Marriott just south of Yonge. By the time she walked there, he would have the room booked.

"Oh, and Dolan, book it in your name for two people. Tell them that your daughter is checking in before you arrive. Remember, I have no ID on me."

"Okay, and call me back when you're in the room, safe."

"Done." Sarah hung up.

She walked away from the pay phone and sipped hard on her coffee, already feeling more alive.

Things would work out. The government wouldn't be after her anymore. She could rest easy. Hank and Rod were dead, and with the world thinking she was also dead, there would be no more adversaries. She could slip back into her old life and start helping people again—anonymously.

Something Hank said earlier entered her mind. He had called her a 'victim.' Was she? Would it always be about her trying to stay alive? Or could she put together something of a normal life?

She filled her mouth with coffee, swished it around slowly, and let it warm her insides on the way down.

Everything would work out. She would leave Toronto, go home, and start over.

But first, she had to find out who those guys with the white faces were. That kind of slaughter couldn't go unanswered.

And Vivian had some explaining to do.

Chapter 8

SIMON PETER ENTERED THE apartment first. He removed the eviction notice on the door. They were behind in the rent, but where they were going, it wouldn't matter. There were no credit checks in Heaven.

After removing his jacket, he opened the red wine to give it time to breathe before his apostles joined him for communion.

He performed the meticulous task of setting the bread and wine glasses out so that he would be ready for their meeting when they all showed up.

He undressed, slipped into a brown robe, and sat cross-legged in the middle of the living room to pray. After ten minutes, he was so wrapped up in prayer he didn't notice Philip and Andrew enter, followed by Thomas and, a few minutes later, James.

Movement in the kitchen disturbed him. He summed up his final words and asked God to see him through his mission of sending His children home. Then he asked for his brother

Matthew to be more forthcoming, offer more information during their sessions and allow them to continue their mission unimpeded.

"In Jesus' name, amen."

Simon opened his eyes. The apostles stepped into the living room and sat in a circle around him. James held a silver tray with the wine already poured into tiny shot glasses and the bread. As Simon joined the circle, James handed the bread and wine to each man. Once everyone was in position and held their bread and wine, Simon was ready.

He held up the bread. "This is the body of Jesus that was broken for you. Take this bread in remembrance of him." Everyone touched the bread and closed their eyes as Simon had instructed them. They chewed it and swallowed.

He could see the strained look on all their faces. He would have to answer for the death of two of their own soon to maintain control and order.

He held up his wine. "This is the blood of Jesus that was spilled for your sins. Take this wine and drink it in remembrance of him. Let the wine absolve you of sin and allow you free entry into the Kingdom of God."

His apostles tilted their heads back, closed their eyes again, and drank the wine. Their glasses empty, James collected the refuse and discarded it in the kitchen before returning to the circle.

They had no use for furniture. Simon ordered everyone to sleep on blankets as Jesus once did. The apartment was rented as a meeting place. Once the lease was signed, they hadn't paid any rent after the first month. They were due to be evicted within a few weeks, but Simon didn't care. Their mission for God would be over by then.

He examined their eyes, moving along the circle, one by one. It was good to see they had all removed their hairpieces and contact lenses as he'd instructed. They couldn't allow the forces of evil to spot them near this apartment after being seen at the mall.

Philip appeared content, eager to listen to more of Simon's words. Andrew seemed calm, as well as Thomas. After what they had just been through at the Allandale Centre, Simon was elated to see they weren't allowing it to affect them negatively. After all, they worked on divine tasks. No human judgment could render that less powerful. Simon had been quite clear in the weeks leading up to today's outing.

It was James who appeared the most out of sorts. Discontent tensed the lines of his face. Simon allowed James the time to work through his emotions as they discussed what had happened and what they would do to right the wrongs that had been brought upon them.

"My fellow men," Simon started, "we are gathered here today minus two. Our beloved brother, John, has departed for the great hereafter. We mustn't be selfish and mourn his loss. We need to rejoice in the knowledge that he's home, in a better place. He has been taken in the Rapture." Simon scanned their faces slowly as he talked. "We have lost Brother Michael, too. We are further blessed for having worked side-by-side with such loving, caring men, and I thank the Lord for having known them. Please pray for their wonderful reception in the Kingdom."

Simon lowered his head and whispered a prayer for John and Michael. Soft whispers emanated from his fellow brothers. A chorus of amens filled the room as they finished.

"Simon?" Philip asked. "Permission to speak."

"All of you," Simon said, his hands raised, "have permission to speak. Let it out. Tell all. What's on your minds?"

Philip cleared his throat. "Have you heard from your brother Matthew?"

Simon shook his head. "Not yet. But rest assured, Brother Philip, I will."

"Can you tell us what went wrong?" Andrew asked.

"Circumstance." Simon got to his feet. He needed to show them confidence and power. He needed to instill the right words to keep them rooted in faith, and he couldn't do that sitting cross-legged in their circle. "Circumstance halted our mission."

"Circumstance?" James asked, his voice wavering.

"Yes, Brother James. It is unfortunate that Sarah fought back. We didn't expect that much resistance." He was careful not to say he didn't expect it, showing weakness in solidarity. Including them in the expectation made them part of the collapse of the mission. "However, we did expect Sarah to run. We've all read about Ms. Sarah Roberts's good deeds." He talked with his hands, moving them with his words, his Italian blood showing through. "We all know that she is truly one of the good ones. That is why she needs to be taken home to be with our Lord."

"What about all those cops?" James asked. He looked scared now. His eyes darted between his brothers and then back to Simon. Sweat beaded on his forehead. "They have families, wives, children. Is it right what we did?"

Simon glanced around the circle before answering. He needed to see if any of the others were as weak as James. He knew what had to be done. It was time for James to move on. Not only could this kind of weakness get James Raptured in the process of fulfilling his destiny, but he could also get others Raptured early, jeopardizing their mission. James would need to be taken out on the next mission.

"Brother James, let me ask you a question."

James nodded, not willing to talk back to Simon Peter.

"Who are the bad people in society? Who are the ones staying behind for the thousand-year war and the end of the earth by fire?"

"People in jails, people hurting others for pleasure."

"That's right, Brother James," Simon said, keeping as calm as the virgin in her shroud, as calm as a summer sea. His posture, facial expressions, and mannerisms meant everything to his followers. After all the preaching and all the parables he offered, none of them really truly believed in his mission until he showed them, on paper, what Matthew had said. That brought them on board. Simon's job was to keep them rapt in his inner circle, fighting against the winds of evil.

"Who are the good? Who needs to be Raptured and taken home?"

"God is almighty, all-seeing," James said, reciting Simon's teachings. "He is taking home everyone He desires, but a few need our help. He has enlisted us to do his bidding. We're on a mission—"

"That's correct, Brother James, but who can go home?" Simon interjected, trying to get James to mellow out. "Who is authorized to be Raptured by our hands?"

"Good people. Ones that the Lord needs."

"Correct again," Simon said, his arms outstretched.

"Wouldn't you agree that police officers, who protect our women and children, are good people, deserving of Rapture?"

James scanned the room for support and, finding none, looked back up at Simon. "Yes, Brother Simon. I do."

"In the future, examine your questions prior to asking them. Does anyone else want to talk, let it out, and discuss what happened? Discussion is important. Thinking, tantamount."

No one responded.

"Good," Simon said. "I'm going into the other room to call Matthew. We need direction here. Sarah is still our primary goal, and Matthew can tell us what to do. When I get a hold of my brother, I will rejoin the circle and tell you what I've discovered. We will reconvene to make things right. Are we all agreed?"

As Simon moved around the room, each man raised both hands heavenward, palms open and facing the ceiling, allowing God's energy to course down their arms and into their soul, their hearts.

"Good, now pray, talk to God, and then rest. No one leaves. We'll meet when I come out of the bedroom."

In the bedroom, they had an altar set up for those that had passed over. Simon opened a bottle of salve and applied the white cream to the palms of his hands and soles of his feet. The cracking had become something of a pain recently. He would need to be diligent with his skin and fingernails over the next few days to keep them from getting infected. He had lived with ectodermal dysplasia for twenty-four years and had undergone countless doctor visits, dental surgeries for his teeth, and tests. Always more tests.

Before leaving today, he removed the dentures covering the two pointed teeth on the bottom of his mouth. There was no need to be accepted by society, no need to appease the sensitive nature of the common people. God had created him and his brother in his image, and Simon needed to be proud of his appearance. He wouldn't chastise or ridicule himself anymore—he would leave that to the ignorant and less educated.

He sat on a cushion in front of the altar, crossed his legs, placed his upturned hands on his knees, and began to pray.

He would wait for Matthew to call.

The Rapture was upon them, and nothing could stop the Rapturites from sending Sarah Roberts home. She would die by Simon's hand. When Simon changed his name, he also took on the role of bringing people to Jesus. He had every intention to deliver Sarah to God. Even if he died doing it.

There could be no greater honor.

Chapter 9

Sarah entered the hotel Dolan had arranged. At the desk, they gave her no trouble. Dolan had described her and said his daughter had lost her purse. He would join her later but charge what she needed on his card. The young attendant at the counter had been overly nice, offering her candies from a large bowl. He gave her two electronic door lock keycards and explained about the restaurant, the pool, and checkout times. All she wanted was a long hot bath and room service.

After feigning sleepiness, Sarah got away from him without being too rude. She checked in with the name Sarah Ryan, Dolan's last name. Using his name made her feel special after all they'd been through together.

She put out the DO NOT DISTURB flap and secured the night lock. Dolan, or anyone else, wouldn't be joining her this evening.

She grabbed the restaurant menu, ordered room service to be delivered in one hour sharp then drew a hot bath. She disrobed, hopped in the steaming water, and finally relaxed.

She was safe. Only Dolan knew where she was. She could stay the night and decide what to do in the morning. If Parkman were already in the States, maybe she would have to bite the bullet and call her parents. After reassuring them she was alive and well, her father could drive up and fetch her. Until then, she could stay locked up in this hotel.

She sunk lower in the tub, letting the filth of the past week locked in a cell ooze off her. She needed new clothes. Maybe the hotel had a gift shop where she could at least buy a hat and a toothbrush. She was weary, tired of being on the run. It was time to get her life back.

The phone rang. She wondered if it was the kitchen with a question about her food. They could wait. She needed to enjoy her tub before she would eat. She had all night to eat, sleep and eat some more. Which reminded her she needed to order some kind of chocolate dessert. A Snickers cake or double chocolate arrangement of some kind. A woman needed her chocolate.

The phone stopped ringing.

She dipped her dark hair in the water, ran her hands through it, and pushed up and out to grab the small bottle of shampoo.

The phone started again.

"Holy shit, take it easy," she shouted into the room.

She lathered up her hair, trying to stay calm, but the phone didn't stop. Maybe it wasn't the kitchen. If it were, their next step would be to send someone up to knock on her door. She wanted to avoid anyone else seeing her face, so she quickly rinsed her hair, soaped up her body, and rinsed off under the shower.

While towel drying her hair, the phone started again.

She ran out, still naked, and picked up the receiver.

"Is there a reason to keep calling—"

"Sarah, it's me."

"Oh, hey, Dolan. Sorry about that. Thought it was the hotel. I was in the tub. I was supposed to call, wasn't I? Sorry. Everything okay?"

"No." He breathed in deeply, exhaling as if it was his last breath. "They're looking for you."

Her stomach couldn't take anymore. "Who?" Even after she asked the question, she dreaded the answer.

"You didn't tell me what happened at the mall," Dolan said.

"Yeah, long story. Why?"

"A lot of cops died."

She dropped the towel on the bed and swung her hair over one shoulder. She felt vulnerable standing naked, talking on the phone.

"How many?" she asked.

"The news channels are saying nine people died. One unidentified man was wearing white powder on his face, sky-blue contact lenses, and a long overcoat. Six Toronto police officers and two members of the American government. The ninth was a woman. They're calling it a massacre. Never before have so many police officers been killed at one time in one place."

"Rod Howley is dead, too," Sarah said. "The woman's name was Joan Frommer, Hank's wife."

"Sarah, what happened?"

"Can you give me a sec?"

"Sarah ..."

"I gotta get dressed. I jumped out of the tub to take the

call."

"Okay, go."

She set the phone down on the bed. While slipping into her panties, she wondered how much to tell Dolan. He deserved as much of the truth as she knew, but she didn't know much. She decided to slim everything down and stick to only what she knew.

She lay on the bed in her shirt and panties and picked up the phone. "Dolan?"

"Yeah."

He sounded dejected and saddened.

"This wasn't me. It's not my fault."

"I know, Sarah," he said. "You would never be a part of something like this. But they're assembling every officer in Ontario for the largest manhunt in history."

"Hank held me in an underground cell. I wasn't sure I'd ever get out. Apparently, Rod called him and said he had Hank's wife as his prisoner. Rod wanted to trade for me. A meeting was set up for the Allandale Centre. That's how we all came to be there. Hank was prepared. Toronto police were all over the place. Then Hank's wife showed up with some kind of white powder on her face. She had a picture of Rod Howley, dead. She didn't say a word. Very creepy."

"Oh, man …"

"I know. She died in Hank's arms a minute or two later. All I know is these men wearing overcoats and white faces walked around carrying death in their hands—"

"What? Who?"

"Men were wearing the same white paint Joan wore on their faces. Whoever they touched died within seconds. I have no fucking idea what the hell they had in their hands, but it was definitely lethal. Two of them attacked me."

"How did you get away?"

"Cops started falling all around me. The white-faced attackers were closing in. I'm unsure if I was their target because they went after the cops first, but I may have been. I ran to the sporting goods store. They chased me inside. One of them just stared at me and said, 'Come.' Creeped me out."

"And?"

Sarah recounted the rest of the events at the mall to Dolan.

"You killed the one they found?" Dolan asked.

"Yes. Then I ran through the back hallways of the mall, out the door by the garbage compactor, and once I got clear of the mall, I called you. That's it."

"Oh, Sarah, I wish I could help you out of this mess."

"What are you talking about? What mess? I didn't do anything unless escaping with my life is a bad thing?"

"Turn on the news. Any channel you want. It's all anyone is talking about."

"I don't want to see it. I was there, remember? It was traumatic as hell. I just want to forget it."

"Sarah, a man named Detective Waller just did a press conference on the slaughter of his men. He says you started the whole thing. He has your name and video footage of you and said you're armed and dangerous. Your face is all over the news, and every cop on the continent wants your head."

"What? That's ridiculous!" She jumped off the bed. The walls of the room closed in on her. She thought she might as well be dead as the world had thought. "Dolan, is anyone asking how I've been resurrected? What am I going to do? You know I wouldn't partake in—you know I had nothing to do with this. I'd be dead, too, if I hadn't fought back and run. There has to be video footage that would verify that."

"I know. The best thing to do is contact Waller and tell him your side. Explain how Hank had you as a captive and that this was supposed to be a simple trade—"

"That won't work," Sarah said as she paced the floor beside the bed.

"Why not?"

"Because I met Detective Waller, and it didn't go well."

"Oh, Sarah, what did you do?"

"He overheard me telling Hank that I could kill him within seconds if I were challenged. He questioned Hank about me and why I was there. That's when I heard Hank had sold the Toronto cops a bill of goods."

"What are you talking about?"

Sarah stopped pacing. "The Sophia Project men always fabricate what's happening to get local cops involved. Like at the Rogers Centre when I met Drake. Anyway, Hank told them we were waiting for Rod, a sex offender."

"A sex offender? You serious?"

"I wonder what Hank told Waller about me. Maybe that's why he has a hard-on for me. This can't get any worse. "

"Yes, it could," Dolan said.

"How?"

"You could be dead. That would be worse."

"True."

"I can't give myself up. That has never worked in the past. The cops dance to a different beat than I do."

"Sarah, I don't see any other play here. Sure, it'll take a while to work everything out, but at least you'll be protected while inside. Whoever did this couldn't have been after you.

Everyone thought you were dead. Think about it. You're the dead girl. Whatever happened at that mall was about Hank or Rod or someone else, not you. Meet with Waller, tell him everything, and I mean everything. You'll be home by next weekend. Worst case scenario, your parents and I will get a good lawyer to bring you home."

Sarah considered what Dolan was saying. He was right. Everyone had thought she was dead. But why did that man beckon to her through the sporting goods window? It felt like they were after her.

"You know, Dolan, I never thought I'd say this with how I feel about cops in general, but what you're saying actually sounds comforting. You're right. It couldn't be about me. How could it? I was dead as far as anyone knew. Even if it took a couple of weeks to work out, mall security cameras would have pictures of the men in overcoats. They'll be able to see that I was running for my life just like the cops were."

"Exactly. Don't live on the run. This is too big. I'll marshal everyone from this side of the border to help. Don't attempt this on your own."

"I wouldn't be alone. I have Vivian."

"Yeah, but Vivian is there as a conduit to help people in need, not for you to evade the law."

"I'm in need here."

"Call Waller. Arrange a meeting. Don't have all of Toronto after you."

After a few moments, she sat on the edge of the bed, relieved by her decision.

"I will. Hey, did you read any newspaper articles on me this past week?"

"You don't want to hear about that."

"Why not?" she asked, a bit too loud. "Is it going to piss me off?"

"They glamorized you, made you look like a gift from God himself, saving people from certain death, kidnappings, and human trafficking, all at the personal expense of being shot, bones broken, and nearly dying numerous times. You're a national hero right now. Don't sully that by running."

"Shit, I won't. Don't worry. I'll call him right now."

Someone knocked on the door.

"Food's here. Gotta go. Hey, thanks for helping a girl out. I really appreciate it."

"Anytime, Sarah. You're the daughter I never had."

"Ahh, that's sweet. You're one of a kind, Dolan. Gotta run, take care. Life goes on, doesn't it?"

"Yes, Sarah, life goes on."

She clicked off. Another knock at the door, along with a man announcing room service.

She tied her wet hair back and peeked through the peephole. It was the guy from the front counter.

Sarah unlocked the door, opened it a crack, and stuck her hand around the edge. "I just came out of the shower. Can you hand me the plates this way?"

"Yes, ma'am."

A warm plate was placed gently into her hand. She squeezed it through the door, set it on the carpeted floor by her feet, and reached out again. After all the plates were transferred to her, the hotel clerk asked if she needed salt and pepper. She declined and went to shut the door.

"Excuse me, ma'am?"

She stopped the door at the last second. "What is it? And stop calling me ma'am."

"You have to sign for the food, ma—" he caught himself, cleared his throat, and said, "please."

She shook her hand. "Give it to me."

After being handed the receipt and a pen, she signed for the food and handed it back.

"Thank you," he said from behind the door. "Have a good night."

After he left, she locked the door. Then she picked up the three plates and the bottle of red wine off the carpet, carried it to the bed, and dug in.

After a couple of bites of chicken breast and a few large sips of the Australian Shiraz, she grabbed the remote and turned on the TV. Two clicks of the channel, and it landed CP24. They were talking to a woman live at the Allandale Centre. Sarah stopped chewing as this mother of two recalled what had happened.

She lost her appetite when CP24 played amateur clips from someone's cell phone.

The video captured the men in overcoats, but it also showed Sarah running and the window being shot out of the sporting goods store as Sarah dove to the ground.

The news anchor explained that was when the police discovered that Sarah Roberts, previously thought to be dead, was trying to escape and, after repeated warnings, had no option but to shoot at her.

The amateur video continued. They had caught her shoving a man to the ground in the sporting goods store and then running away. The video stopped there, and the news anchor said they couldn't show anymore to keep the man's identity confidential until the police notified the next of kin. The man died from whatever Sarah had touched him with, the anchor reported.

"I was defending myself," Sarah said to the empty hotel room, her stomach churning. She was no longer hungry. "He was trying to kill me," she whispered. "Shit, you guys have that wrong."

She took another bite of her chicken because she had to eat. She had no idea when she would eat such good food again. Detective Waller came on camera and explained that Sarah Roberts was a person of interest and that she was armed and dangerous. He warned anyone who saw Sarah—a picture from the mall cameras came on the screen—to call the police.

"Do not approach her," he said, his face close to the camera. He strained to compose himself. "I repeat, do not approach her."

Sarah had to call him. They needed to talk and make this kind of propaganda go away. She would be marked for the rest of her life if she didn't make it all go away.

She grabbed the phone, but her finger hesitated over the numbers.

"Shit," she said out loud. "The receipt for the food. I signed my real name. Damn." She swiped the half-full plates off the bed, where they clattered unbroken to the floor.

Then she set the phone down and decided to call him after a short nap. She needed to talk to Waller as soon as possible but didn't know when she'd get another chance to sleep.

This was going to hurt, having to work with the police, deal with them, let them charge her if that's what they wanted, and then try to get out from under the umbrella of suspicion.

It was all because of those white-faced assholes. When this was all over, she would exact justice on them.

She needed to live up to the reputation the newspapers had given her.

She didn't play the role of the victim too well.

Chapter 10

Simon Peter picked up a piece of paper from the floor. He read the note over a couple of times. He needed to be clear and ensure the instructions were right in his head. He was their leader and needed to always appear confident and sure of himself and his brother. A unified front.

When he met Andrew at the Pentecostal Church, Matthew had told him that Andrew would be pivotal in reforming the others. Matthew and Simon didn't have a lot of friends growing up because of their ectodermal dysplasia. Andrew had been popular and had many friends, four of whom were in the church. Men who had stuck by him and were devout Christians.

Simon remembered the day he read a note from his brother about Andrew, similar to the one in his hand. Brother Andrew had a skydiving trip planned for later that day with Brother James and Brother Philip. The note had explained that they would all die that day as the Cessna would crash on the runway before takeoff. It would explode as the fuel lines ruptured, instantly killing everyone on board.

After Simon persuaded Andrew with his prophecy, Andrew canceled and convinced Brother James and Philip to cancel as well. They went to the small airport to persuade the pilot to stay grounded, but all he did was perform an extra safety check of his equipment and announce his plane was sound. They packed three first-timers onto the plane for tandem jumps and took off as planned.

The plane encountered trouble at just over fifty feet. By one hundred feet, the pilot tried to turn around, but it was too late. Simon and his new friends watched as the plane hit hard, exploding upon impact. There were no survivors.

They had only told the pilot of their concerns. Since no one else knew about the prophecy, no one asked any questions. It was assumed they were lucky as they had canceled due to the jitters.

Brothers Andrew, Philip, and James watched Matthew's messages come true from that day on. They were all convinced that the messages were divine, and if God had chosen them for this path, then nothing could tempt them from it.

And now the time had come. The Mayans had predicted it, the Bible talked about it, and now the chosen few were standing up and aiding in the Rapture.

Brother John, recently deceased, and Brother Thomas both came aboard with little convincing from Andrew.

The Rapturites had formed and were about to embark on their greatest mission yet: to send home as many righteous people as they could touch before they had to go home themselves.

However, Simon hadn't informed them that the last batch

of syringes were for the Rapturites. They thought they were gifted, protected, and would continue working for God for quite some time. The truth was, as soon as Sarah Roberts was dispatched, the Rapturites would be no more.

For Simon, it was all about Sarah. She couldn't be allowed to use her automatic writing abilities anymore. Her reign was over, and Simon intended to be the one who ended it.

He collected himself, adjusted his robe, and stepped into the living room. His remaining four brothers sat in various states of prayer—Andrew by the balcony door, Philip near the kitchen, and James and Thomas side by side on the living room floor.

"Brothers," Simon whispered so as not to jar them out of their moment with God. One by one, they roused and turned to him. He reveled in the power, the recognition. He'd been an afterthought his whole life. His parents were lower-educated slobs living on the system who did nothing with themselves. Health care in the States required money, something his parents drank away or shot in their veins. Growing up with their condition, Simon and his brother had hidden from the world until the day they killed their parents in their drunken sleep and got away with it. Now they were free to do God's bidding.

"Everyone, gather around. I have heard from my brother."

He leaned his back against the eggshell-white wall and lifted the note.

"A man named Dolan Ryan has come to Sarah's aid. I'm going to need you, Thomas, to drive down to the States and offer Dolan Ryan a pass homeward. If he is helping Sarah, then he's one of the good ones, and God will need him. I have his address and an address for a woman named Esmerelda. Matthew didn't explain her connection, only that she is to go home as well."

Brother Thomas nodded. "It shall be done. Praise the Lord."

"That's not it," Simon cautioned. "There's more."

"I'm listening," Thomas said.

"While we remain here and help Sarah on her way, not only will you attend to Dolan and Esmerelda, we need you to go to Sarah's hometown and send her parents heavenward. Having raised such a good person, we can't leave Sarah's parents behind to face the coming Armageddon. Are you able to handle this task?"

Thomas nodded. "Willing and able. I will do as instructed by the good Lord, hallelujah."

"You will be provided with all the pertinent addresses, a car, five syringes, and enough money to make it south, one way."

"Five syringes?" Thomas asked.

Simon smiled, making sure to keep his lips sealed. "Brother Thomas, we're counting on you to handle Dolan, Esmerelda, and then both of Sarah's parents with the first four syringes. After that, the last one will be to send you home. God is awaiting you, personally."

"But, Brother Simon, I thought we would be acting for God for some time to come ..."

Simon stepped closer to him. To Thomas's credit, he didn't move. "Don't let your flesh and blood rank higher than your divinity."

"I'm sorry—"

"Self-preservation is for the weak, the sinners. The Kingdom of God is glorious. We are directly serving Him, working for Him. When your employer calls you home, and it's the almighty Lord Himself, you answer the call." He waved his arm in a sweeping motion. "All of you have been chosen. You are the elite, trusted with His mission, His goals." Simon turned back to face Thomas. "While you take a day or two to complete your final mission," he shook the paper in his hand, "we'll be completing ours. By the time you are Raptured, we will be, too. Do not," he raised his voice as if on the pulpit, "I repeat, do not be sent home by the bullet of the evildoers. There won't be time to bless you. Entering the Kingdom will become a hardship one wouldn't care to burden oneself with. Go your own way. Inject at the end." He slapped his hands together. "We all must inject at the end."

Brother Thomas stepped forward until he was no more than one foot from Simon.

"I accept this divine mission and will complete it at all costs."

"Praise the Lord," Simon said, raising his hands above his head. "We will pray for you, Brother Thomas."

"Then I will see all of you in the home of our Lord."

Simon turned his attention to the other three brothers. "Our next meeting will be at His table. We are invited to a feast, but first, we have business here in Toronto. Sarah is downtown in a hotel. I don't have the exact hotel. Some of Matthew's information is being blocked, but I have the information we need to send her home successfully. We need to plan this together and then leave at once. A Detective Waller will be visiting her shortly. We're to report to the corner of Yonge and Bloor Streets. There's supposed to be an accident after nine p.m. this evening, and Sarah will be present, as will we."

Andrew raised a hand. "Can you tell us why Matthew is being blocked?"

Simon shook his head. "It's unprecedented. I can't explain it. All I know is that we have all the information we need to execute God's plan. Are we ready to finish this?"

The apostles nodded in unison.

"Good. Now, Brother Thomas, let's get you ready and send you off first. Then the rest of us can head downtown. It's time to send Sarah Roberts home and finish this. The end is near. The Rapture is upon us, and we're the chosen few. Isn't it a glorious day?"

Simon saw the doubt in James's eyes, but he knew James wouldn't last the night. Matthew had explained that James would be killed during tonight's accident.

Oh, it's going to be a glorious evening.

Chapter 11

SARAH SLEPT INTO THE early evening, woke up, and grabbed
the phone. She had to call Waller and set up a meeting.

She dialed and got transferred through to Detective
Waller's cell phone after five minutes of struggling to get
past the gatekeepers. They said he was too busy to take
personal calls. Then she was told he was simply too busy,
even though Sarah explained that she was the one Waller was
looking for. Finally, the last woman she talked to wanted to
check the veracity of her statement. Sarah told the woman to
ask Waller what food stand he had stood inside to ward off
the men in overcoats. Once her facts were verified, Waller
answered.

"Sarah Roberts?" he asked, his voice as deep as she
remembered.

"Detective Waller. You've pissed me off."

"How's that?"

Sarah got off the bed to scrounge the rest of her clothes.
The police would trace the call and be on their way. If this

conversation didn't go her way, she wouldn't be here when they arrived.

"You announced to the world that I'm a person of interest. You let them show a clip of me defending myself from those murderers but made it look like I was the aggressor. You were there. You saw as well as I did what happened. I had nothing to do with it. In fact, the only reason I'm not in custody is that I ran for my life, as you did."

"Hank Frommer and his team informed me that we were there to apprehend a sex offender. When those men entered the scene … well, let's just say you were a prisoner of Hank Frommer's, and now you're free. It all adds up. Come on in so we can talk about it."

"I wasn't a prisoner. Hank had snatched me, kidnapped me. I have proof. Ask Drake Bellamy. We were having dinner a week ago at the Old Spaghetti Factory on the Esplanade when Hank stormed in and took me. There was a scuffle—"

Waller cleared his throat. "Can't do that."

"Why not?"

"If we're talking about the same Drake Bellamy, he was found face up in Lake Ontario yesterday morning."

Sarah sat heavily on the edge of the bed. "What? No way. He was a fighter."

"A fellow cop did the ID."

"Spencer?" she guessed.

"Yeah, how did you know?"

After all Drake had been through in the past two months —the Hungarian murderer and then Elmore Ackerman …

"Sarah?" Waller broke through.

"What?"

"We have to meet."

Her head cleared for a moment. She would grieve later. Even though she didn't really know him, she still felt a certain loss. "Why the campaign against me? I ran. You saw that. Those men came after me, too. I pricked one with whatever they had in their hands in the sporting goods store. A female employee saw the whole thing. I'm clean of this. Everything I did was in self-defense."

Outside noise, like a car going past him, made his voice unintelligible.

"What did you say?" Sarah asked, heading for the bathroom.

"I have a lot of good men who died today. It's a fucking zoo around here when a cop is killed in the line of duty, but when this many are killed, the force goes nuclear, looking for answers. I'm your only hope. Come in, sit down, and tell me everything. Let me keep you for a couple of days to guarantee your safety, and then you can head home, providing you actually have nothing to do with those guys."

"And if I don't come in?"

"There are thousands of cops who will hunt you down for a long time just to get the answers I'm looking for. There would be an accident …" he trailed off. "Look, Sarah, if you leave, it looks bad. You know how this works. What the media showed tonight on camera makes you look guilty. Meet with me. Then I can clear your name, and you're free to go."

She stared at herself in the mirror. She hated cops and how they operated. If they could only trust her for a change. That she would have anything to do with what happened at the mall was preposterous.

"Do I need a lawyer?"

"Only if you want one. I won't advise against it, but you're not being charged with anything at this time."

"Do you know if Officer Parkman is still in Toronto? He was helping Spencer, Drake, and me last month on the Elmore Ackerman thing."

"I looked him up yesterday when Hank called to tell us about the Allandale Centre meeting. Hank said you would be there, even though you were supposed to be dead. I had questions no one could answer. Parkman had just gone to your funeral and was headed back to Toronto to look into what had happened. All I know is that he's hanging around somewhere, supposedly looking for you."

She had no choice. She had to meet Waller. She would be safe in the police station. Running in this situation would not work.

"Okay. Find Parkman for me, and I'll come in."

"No, you need to come in now. We can find Parkman later when you're secure."

She thought about it for a second and realized it would be better to get this over with.

"Fine, but I only meet with you. You do the pickup alone."

"Why? I was coming alone anyway."

"I don't trust cops. If I see uniforms, I'm gone."

"It's safer this way. Tell me where you are, and I'll come to get you."

"I'm at the Courtyard by Marriott hotel on Yonge, just north of the Allandale Centre. How long before you can get here?"

"On my way. Be there in ten minutes, say around ten minutes to nine."

"I'm warning you, Waller. No surprises." As an afterthought, she added, "And no handcuffs. Sick of those fuckin' things."

"Fair enough."

He clicked off.

What have I done?

Chapter 12

SIMON SENT BROTHER THOMAS on his way in Brother Andrew's car. He would be at Dolan's before the next morning. By tomorrow evening, Esmerelda and Sarah's parents would be sent home. Everything was coming together better than he thought.

They ordered a taxi an hour ago and now walked around the Toronto Public Library, a block from Yonge and Bloor. Simon's watch said 8:47 p.m.

"It's almost time. Does everyone have their needles ready?"

Philip, Andrew, and James all nodded.

"Good. Tonight will be a glorious night."

"I have a question," James asked.

"Go ahead, my brother."

"When Sarah has been sent home, are we going to, you know?"

"I have no further instructions from Matthew. That tells me our mission is over. Unless he contacts me within the next," he made an exaggerated pull on his sleeve to check his watch, "ten minutes or so, we use the final syringes on ourselves. Gentlemen, tonight we dine with the Lord."

"Hallelujah," Andrew and Philip said in unison.

"Hallelujah," James chimed in a moment later.

"Okay, let's go inside the library and use the washroom to get ready. Use the extra syringes in your pockets if anyone tries to stop us. This mission cannot be a failure. Sarah Roberts is our target, and we have foreknowledge of where she'll be in fifteen minutes, praise the Lord. Let's do this right."

The apostles followed Simon into the library, where they applied the rice powder paste, donned their toupees and contact lenses, and prepared for their last battle on earth.

Chapter 13

SARAH WAS DRESSED AND ready to go within minutes. She stood by the hotel room window, looking down at Toronto at night. Too bad she couldn't explore and tour the city like regular folk. Too bad she couldn't tour it with Drake.

Her eyes glazed over. She had felt something for Drake and considered getting more serious with him. She wondered if his death had anything to do with her. Could it have been the men from the mall? Did all those cops die because some rogue band of hitmen were hunting her? She leaned toward that assumption after the ugly one had motioned for her to come to him.

She shuddered, knowing she couldn't begin to believe that, though. Too many dead to be on her conscience. She wouldn't shoulder that weight.

Her hand went numb for a moment.

"What's does that mean?" she said to the empty room. "Why keep making my hand numb, Vivian?"

Then she passed out.

A moment later, Sarah awoke, her hand sore. The hotel stationery and pen sat on the floor beside her. She flipped the thin pad over and examined the message from Vivian.

After the accident, stand in the middle of the intersection. Shut your eyes. Do not waver. Do not move. Do not use the gun. Kill no one. Be the victim. Do this, or you will die. I can't save you otherwise. There is no other choice. I'm sorry.

Sarah let the note slip from her hand.

After the accident … stand in the middle of the intersection?

"Suicidal much? How am I supposed to do that? And for what?"

Don't use the gun? Kill no one?

"What gun? Kill who?"

She looked around the room as if Vivian was there with her.

"I have no play here, do I? Just offer myself up. Stand in the middle of a busy intersection … fuck!"

She fixed her shirt, straightened her pants, and left the hotel room. The stairs would be faster. On the first floor, she looked out the side exit, saw no one waiting, and then headed down the long hallway of the first floor.

Near the lobby, she slowed. If Waller showed up with a bunch of cops, it would only mean he couldn't be trusted, and Sarah would not go with him.

A woman sat on one of the couches with her son, who looked about six or seven years old. The woman checked her watch and then stared at the windows.

Sarah moved into the lobby.

"Can I help you with anything?" the same clerk asked.

"No, I'm fine. Just meeting friends for a drink." Then she

added to the story set in place by Dolan. "Before my father arrives."

"Well, if you need anything, Sarah Roberts …" he paused to let her name sink in. "Just let me know."

She stared at him. With every cop for a thousand blocks wanting to get his hands on her, she wondered if the clerk did something stupid and called them.

"Yeah, I know," he said. "Surprised, eh? Read about you last week in our Toronto paper. Congratulations on all that you've done for everyone." He clapped his hands softly. "You're quite the hero around here. It's an honor to meet you." He leaned in and looked around conspiratorially, a hand half covering his mouth. "I don't believe their version of events at the mall, either. You're too good for that."

He stood back to his full height and adjusted his jacket, smiling, proud of himself for figuring it all out.

She had no idea how to handle adoration. She wanted to slap him for exposing her. She wanted to scream at him because he had no idea how dangerous her life had been, how many people had died in her past, and how many times she had been shot and almost killed.

But most of all, she felt sick. The media glamorized the violence she lived with every day. It was her choice. Vivian worked with her. She felt duty-bound to help, but she wanted obscurity, not popularity.

She would have to go on the road when this was done. She would travel to places where no one knew her. It would be better. For everyone.

She forced a smile and walked to the swinging door. She stepped into the cool evening a moment later and took a deep breath.

Yonge Street bustled at this hour. Construction signs were posted everywhere. She had read something about how all the construction in Toronto drove everyone crazy.

She stepped off the front steps to let a couple with their two kids enter the hotel, dragging their luggage behind them. The little boy had wide, round eyes. He yawned as he stepped past Sarah.

She smiled inwardly, her resolve building. That was why she did what she did. So little boys and girls everywhere could sleep better and safer at night. Damn the media. Damn the hype. She would do Vivian's bidding until it killed her. She believed in the afterlife, so she had nothing to lose. Vivian had shown her the truth. If anything happened to Sarah, she would join her sister.

A small group of teen boys slowed as they looked her up and down. When the sidewalk in front of her thinned of people momentarily, the gang stepped into the road and set something on the circular sewer grate. They stepped back to watch whatever it was they had done.

Sarah moved forward to get a better view. What looked like a silver blade stuck up at a forty-five-degree angle, aimed at the vehicles driving north on Yonge Street.

She looked left. The light had changed half a block down. Two rows of cars, headlights blinding her, approached. She lunged forward, ignoring the shouts from the gang of teenagers, and tried to get to the grate before the first car.

She didn't make it. A red Buick, coming too fast ahead of the other cars, forced her back. She lost her balance and fell into the side of the car as it passed, but caught herself from sprawling out into the street in time.

The Buick's front right tire hit the blade seven feet from

Sarah. The puncture popped like gunfire. The car swerved left, then right, sliding sideways in the street. It came to a stop without hitting anything, half a block up.

People all around gaped. Some had jumped back from the edge of the sidewalk, putting their backs to the wall of the hotel. Southbound traffic had stopped. A horn blared, then another.

The driver of the Buick got out and examined his ruined tire. Then he shot an accusatory glance at Sarah.

She searched for the gang of teenagers. Almost a block away already, they laughed and high-fived each other. She contemplated running after them, calling the police, and holding them accountable, but she couldn't. There just wasn't enough time in the day to deal with all the assholes she encountered.

She waited a moment, got her breathing under control, and then moved down the sidewalk in the other direction. At the corner of the hotel, she slipped into the shadows and waited for Waller to pull up, her hands repeatedly tightening into fists and then releasing.

Lately, her life didn't seem to want to slow down. A month ago, she was held captive by a demented psychopath. Last week it was Hank Frommer and his forced prophecy sessions. Now Hank was dead, Rod was dead, the psychopath was dead, and so was Drake.

She looked at the ground.

What happened to Drake?

She only hoped it had nothing to do with her. It couldn't be. Together they had silenced Drake's enemies. She'd helped free him of the target on his back. If the target had been replaced because of her help, it would be as ironic as getting hit by an ambulance.

She had to change her way of thinking. Negative thoughts were cancerous. Making herself accountable for actions that were meant as good, with no ill intent, was wrong. Thoughts like that would make her judge herself and cause her to slow down what progress she had made. It would be counterproductive. She had to stay strong and always move forward without thinking about repercussions as long as she meant to do what was right. As long as she came from the right place.

Even if that meant she had to walk in front of a car in an intersection as Vivian told her to do.

She pulled Vivian's note out and reread it.

"This sucks sometimes."

She put the note away and watched the people of Toronto walk by on the sidewalk a few feet away, relishing their diversity. Members of almost every culture came and went. A living, breathing melting pot. Maybe Toronto would be a good place to hide out and spend a few years. No one in the States needed her. She'd miss her parents and friends from the now-defunct psychic fair, but maybe she could make a life for herself in the Great White North.

A siren blared from her left. She stepped out to see if it was Waller arriving. A black and white drove by, stopping to deal with the Buick. The cop got out of his cruiser, placed a hat on his head, and walked up to the driver, who still stood by the hood of his car. Southbound traffic had started moving again, but it was slow going. Northbound was eking by around the trunk of the Buick.

As Sarah watched, the driver pointed at her. The cop glanced over his shoulder. She edged back into the shadows.

Now what?

After a couple of breaths, she peeked around the corner again. The cop was halfway to her. She would have to tell him about the teenage boys. They were at least five minutes away by now. It wouldn't sound good, but she couldn't leave her spot as Waller would show any moment. It wouldn't bode well if she weren't here when he arrived.

The cop stepped in front of her.

"Please step away from the wall," the cop ordered.

Sarah moved out of the shadows.

"Why did you try to run into traffic when that car was going by?"

"I didn't try to run into traffic."

"That's not what the driver claims. Just before his tire blew, he said he saw you running at his car, bending down, and then his tire went."

"It was a blade—"

"A what?" the cop cut her off.

She met his gaze. "A group of teenage boys set a blade in the sewer grate over there and stepped back. When I realized what they were doing, I ran to the street to remove the blade, but it was too late."

The cop nodded in an exaggerated fashion. "Right. Okay. And where are these teenage boys now?"

She could tell he wasn't buying her brand of truth but felt compelled to answer his question.

"They ran that way," she said, pointing north.

"Okay, normally, a flat tire doesn't bother me," the cop said. "But when it looks like deliberate sabotage on such a busy street, that gets under my collar. You'll have to come with me and give a statement."

"I can't." She glared at him.

He pushed his chest out subtly, his alpha-male complex genuinely surprised.

"Excuse me?"

"I said I can't. I'm not leaving with you."

"And why's that?"

"I'm waiting for the police to pick me up." She looked around his shoulder on each side, but no Waller yet. She hoped he would show up soon because trouble was brewing.

"Oh, this just keeps on getting better. And why would the police be picking you up?"

She gave a quick smile for his benefit and then looked away.

"Did you hear what happened earlier today at the Allandale Centre?" he asked.

She nodded, afraid her answer would upset him more.

"Police officers were slaughtered."

"I'm sorry."

"You're sorry?" His voice raised a notch. "You're sorry? Understandably, that incident this morning makes the rest of us police officers a little uneasy on the job today."

"I would be."

She tried to move around him as he blocked her view of the street. Waller could park and walk into the hotel without her even seeing him. He countered her move. This was getting annoying.

"Is that a threat, miss?"

"Look," Sarah said. "I told you what happened. A group of teenagers set it up as a prank. They fled north on this street. I tried to help but got there too late. Now, if you would, allow me to see the street better as I'm waiting for

Detective Waller to show up—"

"Detective Waller?"

"You know him?"

"Know him? He's one of the only cops to walk out of the Allandale Centre alive today." He paused. "Hey, wait a second."

He fumbled with his breast pocket button. He yanked out a notebook and flipped it up. Then he looked from Sarah to the notebook and back again.

Slowly, he replaced his notebook and unclipped his holster. People had gathered in a semi-circle around them. When he touched his holster, a collective gasp came from a few of the female gawkers.

Oh, shit.

"Identify yourself," he said.

She really didn't want to say her name but knew she had to, or things would go from bad to worse.

"Sarah."

"Sarah what?"

She met his gaze. "Sarah Roberts."

He yanked his sidearm out, stepped back, and said, "Sarah Roberts, get on the ground. Hands on the back of your head. Do it now."

"You're making a mistake."

People stepped farther away from them.

"I will shoot if you resist arrest. If your hands come anywhere near me, I will shoot. Get on the ground, now."

Sarah had no option but to listen to him. He would take her to the police station, and Waller would have to talk to her there. The problem was how she would be handled by regular cops who thought she had something to do with their colleagues' deaths.

What now, Vivian? How does this fit into your plan?

"Step away, Officer," Waller's deep voice ordered.

Waller pushed through the onlookers and moved up behind the cop. They looked at each other.

"Afraid I can't do that, Detective. I just caught her in the act of mischief with that Buick over there, and then I identified her from the bulletin earlier. She's wanted for questioning."

"I know. That's what I'm here for. I'm taking her in. Now, lower your weapon and place it back in your holster."

"No."

"What?" Waller asked. "I'm a superior officer, and I'm ordering you to put your service revolver away."

"Friends of mine died today. This bitch was on camera running from the scene with her black-coated friends helping her escape. I got the collar. She's coming with me."

The cop stepped inside her personal space. Before she could react, he dropped to his knees, his firearm aimed at the sky as Waller used some kind of Chuck Norris move in less than a second.

Waller moved his hands so fast that Sarah didn't see exactly what he did, but the cop's gun was taken from his grip and snapped apart, the magazine flying in the air where Waller's free hand caught it. He tossed the empty weapon on the sidewalk a few feet away. Then he lifted his foot off the back of the cop's knee.

The cop had tears in his eyes. It wasn't because of any pain Waller inflicted in those couple of seconds.

"But we lost good men ..." he hiccupped, "men we served alongside."

"I know. But this isn't the way to handle it. Sarah is coming with me. Collect your weapon and collect yourself. Then get back in your cruiser and finish your shift. When you're done, go home, and take a couple of days off. Rest. Don't come back until you remember to earn and honor rank. We work as a team out here. Anything less, and people die. Got it."

The defeated cop lowered his shoulders and nodded. He picked up his sidearm and its pieces and shuffled to his car, only looking back at Sarah one more time.

"Come on," Waller said. "Let's go."

Waller led her through the throng of onlookers that were starting to disperse. He opened the passenger door of a Ford F-150, waited until she hopped in, and then closed the door behind her. Once behind the wheel, he flipped off his hazards and turned into the northbound traffic to go around the Buick.

"What was that all about?" he asked.

Sarah pegged him for late twenties or early thirties. No wedding ring and no wrinkles. A flat stomach. She admired discipline. Not many people had it.

"Just a bunch of teenagers fooling around."

"Tell me."

Waller maneuvered his pickup around the trunk of the Buick. The driver was on his cell phone, probably calling a tow truck, while the cop stood beside him and watched Sarah as they passed. She kept her eye on him in case he tried something foolish.

"They stuck a knife in the sewer grate's little hole where water runs down. I saw what they did and ran to yank the knife out, but I got there too late. The driver saw me and thought I had something to do with it."

Waller glanced sideways at her, then back at the road.

"You always try to play the hero?"

"No. Shit just happens in front of me. I'm like a shit magnet."

Waller chuckled. "You remind me of the Trailer Park Boys."

She turned to him. "Trailer Park Boys? Should I be taking that as an insult?"

"No, no, it's a Canadian TV show. They film it in the Maritimes. You just reminded me of one of the characters when you said shit magnet."

"Hmm," she mumbled. "Lovely."

They drove in silence for a moment. As she remembered what Vivian had said, Sarah broke out in a clammy sweat. She was to step into the middle of an intersection after the accident. What accident? Could it have been the Buick? Did she miss her chance?

What now?

"You okay?" Waller asked.

"Yeah, fine," she tried to sound normal as she rubbed her hands up and down the legs of her pants.

"We haven't got far to go," he said. "Don't worry. We'll get to the bottom of this."

That sounded weird to her. What could he mean? Was Waller taking her to the police station or somewhere else?

"What did you do back there to that cop?" Sarah asked. "You were fast."

"Shotokan."

"Shotokan," she said, hearing the word for the first time. "What's that?"

"A little-known martial art. Only a few practice it. It's

great for people like you."

"Why?"

"Because it's designed for street fighting, too. All you need is the strength of your thumb to bring down some big guys. Women fare better with Shotokan."

They approached a red light at a busy intersection. Bloor Street.

"I'll have to look that up—"

A loud ping cut her off. The truck swerved hard right. Waller yanked on the wheel, pulling the pickup off the edge of the sidewalk and back onto the road. The truck moved left, and for all the effort Waller exerted on the steering wheel, he couldn't turn it back.

Sarah braced for impact. A black H2 Hummer had just turned right off Bloor, heading south on Yonge, when Waller's pickup crossed all the lanes of Yonge Street and headed straight at it.

They hit the grill of the Hummer, shoved it onto the sidewalk, and nose-first into the front window of a nail salon hard enough just to break the glass window in the front.

Waller lay in his seat, his head resting on the back. Blood trickled from his forehead where he had hit the steering wheel. Sarah checked his pulse. Strong and steady.

She turned the pickup's engine off, pulled the keys, and tossed them on the carpet by his feet. She grabbed his weapon and opened the pickup's door.

The Hummer driver was just getting out.

Sarah ignored him as she slipped the gun into the back waistband of her jeans and continued walking.

The teenage boys stood by the corner, watching what they had done this time, mouths open.

Sarah pulled the gun out as she headed for the intersection. She fired above their heads, making them think she was aiming at them. They ran away like their asses were on fire.

She replaced the weapon in her waistband, stepped into the middle of the intersection at Yonge and Bloor, and ignored the shouts of passersby as a vehicle from each side came at her. The light changed to yellow. Both cars revved their engines to make the light.

"You better be right about this, Vivian, or I'll see you in a few seconds."

Chapter 14

THE COUPLE IN THE back seat couldn't keep their hands off each other.

Mike had picked up the fare on Blue Jay Way by Roger's Centre and was taking them to an office party at the Xerox Centre on Bloor. The woman was hot, dressed in a tight red miniskirt. Her low-cut blouse left nothing to the imagination, the bottom of the V-neck just above her belly button.

As far as Mike could tell, she enjoyed the attention her partner lavished on her. Numerous possibilities ran through his mind on the ride. Was she an escort or his new girlfriend? Whatever she was, she was hot, and Mike didn't get a lot of fares as pretty as her unless he got the calls for the strip clubs in town after they closed. Seemed like he was always one of the last ones to the clubs, though, missing the better-looking girls. He always ended up with the dancers who were drunk or high.

He tried to keep his eyes on the road. He wanted to give them privacy in his cab, but movement in his rearview mirror pulled his gaze toward the back seat time and again. Two blocks back, as the man leaned across her stomach and lowered below the seat, the woman had met Mike's gaze in the mirror. Her top had sat open, both perky breasts completely exposed, sitting up at attention.

Mike had yanked his eyes away fast. He'd expected to be chastised and screamed at for being a pervert. But none of that happened. Instead, when he looked back in the mirror, the woman smiled at him, moaned, licked her lips, and rolled a finger around her nipple.

Mike's erection pushed to be released from his tight jeans. For the last two blocks, all he could do was stare in the mirror at the half-naked woman in the back seat of his cab while her male partner did something to her lower region. She stared back at Mike, teasing him, tempting him, asking him to join her with the look in her eyes.

It was all he could do to watch the road. The intersection of Yonge and Bloor was coming up. He had a green light. As soon as he was through the light, he would have to pull over and let his fare out. This was his last chance to memorize the beauty in the back seat of his cab for later.

He looked in his mirror. She had both hands up, rolling her nipples between her thumb and forefinger, moaning even louder. She smiled and blew him a kiss. Mike smiled back.

The light at Yonge changed to yellow. Even though he didn't want to end this ride too soon, he could still make the light. Either that or jam the brakes on and knock the guy in the back seat around.

He hit the gas. Just as he was about to enter the intersection, he looked in his mirror at the woman again.

That was when she screamed.

Not in ecstasy.

In fear.

***

Justin Flannagan was sick and tired of doing what he was told. Anna could go screw herself. She had cheated on him. After three years together, all she ever wanted to do was control him and sleep behind his back.

"Change this, change that," he said out loud to the empty car. "Why do you say it like that?" he said, mimicking her voice in a high nasal pitch. "Why can't you be normal like other guys? Fuck normal, and fuck you, Anna. I'm so done."

Three years and all he got was control, nagging, and bitching. Then he came home early, and she had two guys in their bed. She chased him out to his run-down pickup truck in her bathrobe, shouting about how it wasn't what he thought. She could explain everything.

"Yeah, right. Explain that?" he had yelled after her. "There's no explanation that'll ever make sense. We're through. It's over."

He'd jumped in his pickup and drove. It had been twenty minutes, and she had tried his cell phone seven times so far. He resolved to throw his cell out the window if she tried again. It was old and filled with pictures of her. Her image was on his screensaver and lock screen. He needed a new one anyway.

"Go ahead, whore, call me again. Call me one more time, and I'll fucking throw this phone out the window. You will never see me again, bitch."

He continued west on Bloor, heading to the House of

Lancaster. It was time for a little pussy for himself. He was going to get lap dance after lap dance on the bitch's credit card. He'd already taken the maximum cash withdrawal on her card at the ATM. Now, with Anna's money, he would buy pussy, and no one would stop him.

Then he planned a late dinner. Maybe he would get a massage at a parlor on her credit card. They take credit. He'd checked. Later, when Anna got the card's statement, she could see what he had done.

"Serves you right, bitch," he yelled at his phone on the passenger seat. "You'll learn to fuck with me."

He slammed the steering wheel as his eyes glazed over. Up ahead, the light changed to yellow.

His cell phone rang. He hit the gas to make the light and picked up the phone. Anna's picture told him she was calling again. He turned to throw it out the window.

He entered the intersection to someone screaming at him just outside his window.

Then he was airborne.

***

Simon Peter and his fellow apostles watched as Waller's F-150 collided with the Hummer. They recognized Sarah as she stepped out of the passenger side, walked a few feet, fired a gun in the air, and then hid it behind her.

She continued walking toward them.

In their black overcoats, hiding by the unlit wall area nearest a corner of the intersection, it would be nearly impossible for her to see them.

"This is it, my brothers," Simon said as he stared into the

eyes of each one of his followers, the surprise evident on their faces. Every time Matthew's information proved correct, even though it had saved their lives in the skydiving plane crash, they were stunned. "We all have our needles. It is time to Rapture Sarah Roberts. As it is written, it will be done. Spread out and run to the four corners. We advance as one and come at her in a way that she cannot escape again. We cannot fail our Lord. Now go."

His brothers ran away, preparing for the end of Sarah Roberts.

The moment had finally come. He felt overjoyed with glee. His toupee firmly in place, white powder paste hiding his fair skin, Simon waited while his apostles got into position. Sarah continued up the middle of Yonge Street, heading directly for the intersection of Yonge and Bloor.

She must be dazed from the accident, as she didn't veer to the sidewalk. For some strange reason, she continued past the pedestrian crossing on Yonge, between two cars waiting at the red light, and moved into the middle of the intersection.

Simon looked both ways. A taxi cab was coming from the west toward her back. A pickup truck was coming from the east.

Aghast, Simon turned back to Sarah, who now stood in the center of the road.

The light changed to yellow. Both the pickup and the taxi hit the gas to make the light.

Sarah didn't move.

"No," Simon yelled as he ran toward her.

From the corner of his vision, he saw his apostles running at her, too. It appeared Brother Andrew and Brother

James were going to get to her first.

Simon saw the needle sticking out of Brother James's hand as he jumped at her from five feet away.

Sarah didn't notice. Her eyes were closed.

From Simon's vantage point, he saw the taxi driver realize that people were on the road, but it was too late. He swerved to miss Sarah and spun sideways, his bumper sliding past Sarah by no more than half a foot and smacking dead on into James's legs. Brother James had been in the act of jumping at Sarah so that he could jam the needle into her neck when the cab hit him sideways. He catapulted onto the taxi's trunk, his head exploding red spray out the top as he continued in an uncontrolled sideways summersault. He landed on the road on the other side of the cab as the taxi's wheels caught something on the road and flipped sideways.

Brother Simon stopped running and jumped back out of reflex just as the pickup truck barreled past him, doing at least seventy. It spun away from Sarah and hit the backside of the taxi, raising the pickup's front end in the air.

Someone screamed.

The pickup's engine revved high as it flew over the back of the taxi. Brother Andrew had been running into the street beside Brother James. He had dodged the taxi's approach and stopped to stare at the inert form of Brother James on the asphalt.

The front bumper of the airborne pickup connected with Brother Andrew's chin, lifting him in the air and almost decapitating him. When Brother Andrew landed on the concrete, Simon could tell he was dead.

***

The engines of both vehicles revved as they approached Sarah at the intersection. She closed her eyes and waited. Every part of her screamed to run. She wanted to open her eyes, to get to safety, but she had to fight her urges. When Vivian told her to do something, she didn't ask why. She had saved countless lives listening exactly to every word Vivian had offered. Now it was time to save her own.

Vivian wouldn't ask Sarah to kill herself. That couldn't be what this was about. Her sister had inside information, and when Sarah signed on for this automatic writing thing almost six years before, she didn't come aboard half-heartedly. She jumped on with both feet and was fully committed.

That commitment allowed her to not only stand still and keep her eyes closed while her primal urges begged her to run but also smile.

It's all in how you face it, she thought.

Tires screeched behind her somewhere. Her reflexes ordered her to spin on her heels, duck, and move out of the way. Anything but standing in the middle of the road.

But all she did was open her eyes. She barely had time to register the back end of a taxi brush by her leg, ruffling her pants. People on the sidewalk stood open-mouthed, watching.

The pickup truck ten feet away bore down on her. She barely had time to scream as she stepped sideways to the right, out of its path. The driver must've seen the taxi sliding at him, but it was too late. The pickup hit the backside of the cab and rose in the air, hitting a man who had been standing behind Sarah. It momentarily lifted the man off his feet by his head. The man dropped to the ground, his head barely attached.

The pickup landed on all four wheels and skidded to a halt. Sarah's knees unhinged. She dropped to the pavement, shook her head to rid her mind of the images, and then looked up at the black overcoats.

The man who got hit in the head had been right behind her.

His face was white, covered in powder.

They're here.

She spun and checked her surroundings. If one of those white-faced men got too close, she would die. She knew this and now understood what Vivian had done. By standing in the road, two vehicles speeding to make a yellow light had collided. That accident had taken out an attacker.

She got to her feet, legs shaking.

Another man in an overcoat lay on the concrete, his head leaking dark liquid.

Correction. Two white-faced men down.

The taxicab's backdoor opened, and a man stepped out on shaky legs. A woman followed, her hair ruffled from the accident. She adjusted her top and pulled up her skirt. The driver of the cab got out and walked around his cab to examine the damage.

The pickup driver exited his vehicle from the other side of the intersection.

Then two men in black overcoats and white faces stood from a kneeling position behind the taxi where they had been examining their friend.

Anger surged through her.

"Who are you?" she asked from a dozen feet away.

"Good evening, Sarah Roberts," the ugly one with the protruding forehead said. "We are the Rapturites. We've come to take you home. Won't you join us?"

"What the fuck?" She took a step back. Then another.

They advanced.

A siren blared in the distance.

She reached for the weapon in her waistband, then remembered what Vivian had said. Sarah couldn't use the gun. She couldn't kill them.

But I can end this right here, right now. I can shoot them in the feet and leave them to the cops.

She brought her hands back to her sides. She had to listen to her sister.

Shit.

The ugly one waved to her. "Come, join us in Rapture. The time is upon us."

"Yeah, sure," she shrugged. "Okay, but first, I gotta go down to the whorehouse and talk to your mother. Looks like you've been a bad boy and stolen her makeup again."

Ugly smiled. He got uglier. She cringed.

"If we miss you now, we'll keep coming. Nothing of this earth can stop us. We fear no one."

"You're an asshole."

"It's because of you that we've done this."

"Don't blame me for you being an asshole. I didn't cover you in asshole dust and force you two to be such idiots." She almost tripped, then righted herself. "You came after me, remember, dickhead."

Sarah kept the distance to ten feet or more as she continued to back down Bloor Street, both men still advancing. Someone yelled at her that she had to stay at the accident scene. Another man had started to follow them, curious about what was happening.

"At the mall earlier today, did you kill all those cops because you have no fear? Is that what this is? Why are you after me in the first place?"

"Because you're one of the good ones. You help people."

"That's your logic for wanting to kill me—I mean, Rapture me?"

"Yes, God only wants the chosen few before Armageddon begins."

She looked skyward. "See what fame gets you?" She sidestepped an idling parked car. The intersection had filled with people wanting to help. It was at a standstill now. The sirens were closer.

"No more running, Sarah. Come to us, and we'll end this."

She passed an opening to a back alley that led between the stores. She stopped walking backward. She looked down at her feet and saw a cell phone lying there. Quickly, she picked it up. Its glass screen was cracked, and one corner was dented, but it looked like it still worked.

"Yeah, okay," Sarah said. "I'll just walk over there and let you kill me. What are you? Fucking crazy, numbnuts?"

She tossed the phone in her pocket and ran down the alley as fast as her legs could pump. At the corner, she turned right. In seconds she was back on Yonge Street, close to where Waller had smashed into the Hummer.

Detective Waller was being helped out of the driver's seat. He hadn't seen her yet.

She pivoted left and started down Yonge as fast as she could, dodging bystanders, hopping over a fire hydrant, and trying to distance herself from the men in overcoats.

Half a block down, she looked back but couldn't see

them anymore.

Farther south, at her hotel where Waller had picked her up, the Buick was attached to a tow truck. They were lifting the front end, getting ready to move it off the street.

She ran through the hotel lobby and hit the stairs. In her room, she ran into the bathroom and threw up in the toilet. She sprawled on the cool tile and breathed deeply, trying to stave off another burst.

She couldn't.

It took three more clenches of the stomach to empty its contents. Her limbs shook, and her stomach ached. She needed energy. She needed food.

The phone in her pocket rang. She pulled it out and saw the cracked image of a pretty girl calling.

Sarah hit the answer button.

"Hello?"

"Who's this?" the girl asked.

"Not saying," Sarah mumbled. "Too worn out to care."

"Then, can you just tell Justin I'm sorry? You can have fun with him if that's what he needs to make things right. But then he should come home."

"Girl, I have no idea what you're talking about."

Sarah hung up the phone and set it on the floor.

She needed to find out who the Rapturites were and what they wanted with her. How could they find her so easily? Are they getting help?

Her arm numbed.

She crawled out of the bathroom and grabbed the pad and paper from the nightstand.

Then she blacked out.

***

She woke to a note written with urgency. Either that or Vivian had channeled through her weakened body, and what amounted to scribbles was all that came of it.

A man named Matthew was working through someone named Simon Peter. Vivian couldn't explain all the details. All she could tell Sarah was that Simon Peter channels his brother.

Simon Peter is an automatic writer, just like Sarah.

"Holy shit."

Sarah deduced the rest. Since she had used her abilities to make things right and help people, she had become known. It had given her notoriety. She guessed this was something Simon wanted and was jealous of her for it. Killing Sarah under some religious guise allowed him to be the only automatic writer out there.

But that was petty. It couldn't be that simple. Something else had to be at play here, and Vivian wasn't offering more. The end of her note said that Vivian was being blocked. There were rules on the other side. She wasn't all-seeing. Her abilities to help were with Sarah and Sarah alone. She could guide her and try to keep her out of harm's way, but in the end, things could still go wrong, like when she was kidnapped four years ago.

"Okay, so now what?" Sarah asked out loud.

Her sister remained silent.

Sarah couldn't stay in the hotel room. She had to be on the move or hide out somewhere until further instructions. Every police officer on the continent would be after her now that she had walked away from Waller's pickup. She left him there unconscious after stealing his gun. The Rapturites were hunting her and had some kind of celestial help, although none of that made sense to Sarah. Could entities work through someone on this plane to do evil?

She answered her own question. There were malevolent spirits that caused violent hauntings and poltergeists. Maybe Simon's connection, Matthew, was angry at Sarah for something.

She yanked the phone book out of the TV stand drawer and flipped through the yellow pages to martial arts. It was just after ten in the evening. She would walk the streets of Toronto for the night, watching her back, not staying in one place too long, and not allowing Simon to catch up to her.

During that time, she would work her way to a Shotokan dojo. After what she witnessed Waller do to that cop earlier tonight, she needed to learn a couple of quick specialty moves to keep those needle-carrying, white-powdered Rapturites away from her.

There was a Shotokan dojo six blocks from her on Jarvis Street.

She collected herself, checked her hair, rinsed her mouth out to eliminate the taste of bile, and left the room, the cell phone in her back pocket and Waller's gun tucked safely in her waistband.

The next time the Rapturites got as close as they did tonight, she would empty Waller's weapon into them.

With her resolve back, Sarah walked through the lobby, grabbed a handful of candies from the bowl on the counter, and hit the street running.

Chapter 15

SIMON AND PHILIP HAD followed Sarah as far as they could along the alley, but when they came out onto Yonge Street, Simon saw Detective Waller getting out of the front seat with the help of two strangers.

Waller looked around, searching for something. Probably Sarah.

Their eyes locked.

Brother Philip nudged Simon's arm. "Where did she go?" he asked.

Simon nodded toward Waller, who hadn't stopped staring, his eyes growing wider.

"You!" Waller screamed, pointing now.

Simon backed away. Philip followed suit.

"You did this," Waller shouted. He struggled against the men supporting his weight.

Simon was close enough to hear Waller telling the men to let him go. He was a police officer, and he needed to arrest someone.

Simon touched Philip's arm. "I think we need to leave. Matthew will come again. We will get Sarah Roberts another time."

Philip nodded, showing his agitation.

Together they walked briskly back up the alley, out the other side, and headed east down Bloor Street away from the accident where a large crowd had collected. Paramedics had already covered the bodies of their brothers.

Simon whispered a prayer for Andrew and James. Philip seconded Simon's amen a moment later.

"We lost many of our friends today," Philip said, near tears.

"We didn't lose them," Simon said. "All that has happened is God has taken them as he will take us soon enough. They were good men who have been Raptured." Philip slowed his pace. Simon turned to him. "Are you okay, brother?"

"What if we're wrong? What if you've been lucky at guessing things, or maybe you actually do have some kind of power to foretell the future." He kicked at a stone with his foot. "It's just, they were my friends. If what we're doing is right and just, why are they being killed and not Sarah?"

"Brother James was weak," Simon said. "Everyone could tell. At the apartment this afternoon, you saw his demeanor. Everyone did."

"He had questions, that's all."

"What kind of questions?"

They started walking again.

"Like what happened to your parents?"

"Brother Philip, do you really want to know my family history?"

Philip turned sideways. "Actually, yes. If I agree to kill people for God, then maybe I deserve a little family story. Humor me while we walk."

Simon raised his forefinger. "Rapture, not kill."

Philip nodded.

"Okay. I'll tell you a condensed family story. But first, we must find a place to take our makeup and toupees off. Deal?"

A police car headed their way. Simon suggested they spit into their hands, remove as much of the paste as possible, and take off their overcoats. They tossed them in the nearest bush as the cruiser drove by, headed toward the accident.

"Let's get out of this area. Waller made us. He might have called it in. They could cordon off this entire area any minute."

They picked up their pace. Within ten minutes, they were crossing the Bloor Street Bridge over the Don Valley Parkway.

They found a little bistro on the Danforth, near Pape Street. They rid themselves of their cosmetics and sat in the back of the bistro. After ordering bread and red wine, Simon started talking.

"My parents were weak in some areas but strong in others. They were deadbeats, really."

"Yeah, but what happened to them?"

"Matthew and I killed them after they killed Matthew."

Philip shook his head, confused. "What?"

"They claimed it was an accident, but Matthew wouldn't stop crying. It was many years ago. My father smothered him. For years, I feared he would kill me too, thought it was because we were so ugly, but he never came after me."

"What did the police say?"

"They were never involved. It was ruled sudden infant death syndrome."

"It was that long ago?"

Simon nodded. "And Matthew has been talking to me ever since."

The waitress approached with two glasses of red wine and a basket of bread.

"Will there be anything else?" she asked.

"We're fine, thank you."

When she was out of earshot, Philip asked, "How do you know what Matthew tells you is true? I mean, that's the kind of question Brother James asked before he was killed."

"Matthew saved your life, didn't he? Matthew also taught us what drug would work the best to Rapture our choices quickly and painlessly. He even told me where I could get all that we needed to complete our tasks."

"I don't know." Philip looked down at his glass, shaking his head slowly.

Simon sipped his wine. "What don't you know, Brother Philip?"

"Everything we've been taught since day one is thou shalt not kill, and yet that's what we're doing. Something doesn't feel right."

"Am I losing my number one man? Are you having issues with your faith? Do you feel your timing is right to question God and all he has given you?"

"No, no, it's not like that," Philip said, raising his head.

"Then what is it?" Simon asked as he ripped a piece of bread off and put it in his mouth.

"I'm only talking out loud. Why is it so hard if we were

meant to Rapture Sarah Roberts? Why can't His will be done?"

"You remember what Sarah is?"

"Yes, an automatic writer."

"Right. What does that mean?"

"Someone talks through her. They've been working together to save people and help people. She's one of the good ones."

"Right again. That's why she's been chosen for Rapture. She's one of the good ones. If Sarah Roberts were evil, we would abandon this mission and hunt others. This is about sending the good ones home. It always has been." He sipped his wine. "Since we started the Rapturites, who has gone home because of us? Police officers and three of our own. All those people fall into the category of good men. All we've done in the eyes of the Lord are good deeds."

Philip nodded. He hadn't touched his wine.

"Drink up," Simon said.

Philip took his first sip.

"Brother Philip, if what we are doing is wrong, think about it. Would Matthew be allowed to talk through me? Would he be allowed to tell me where Sarah would be? If what we are doing is wrong, then that would be murder and would fall under the Ten Commandments. But it isn't. We're on a mission sanctioned by God himself. Otherwise, we wouldn't hear from Matthew at all, and you would be dead from the plane crash."

Philip sipped his wine. Simon moved the basket of bread closer to him.

"It's something like cryptophasia turned up in volume."

"What's cryptophasia?" Philip asked.

"It's a special language twins are known to create, which only they can decipher. We can even walk and move in unison—something our parents don't have."

"Wow."

The waitress turned up the volume on the TV and said something to her coworker about how upset she was with what had happened at the mall earlier.

On the screen, CP24 posted the faces of Simon, Philip, Andrew, Thomas, and James, one by one. The images had been picked up on mall security cameras. They had the identity of one male deceased but weren't releasing it until next of kin were notified. Another was injured and couldn't talk yet. The news reported that the deceased man had syringes on him with a substance that appeared to have killed all the dead at the Allandale Centre.

Even with his toupee off, Simon was aware that the distinctive features of ectodermal dysplasia made him highly recognizable.

"Let's finish these and get out of sight. We can't afford to be held by the police. If something like that happens, we'll miss our opportunity to Rapture Sarah."

Philip nodded and grabbed his glass of wine. Simon could tell he wasn't completely on board, but he wouldn't waste any more time trying to convince him. They would only need one or two more days before they'd get another chance to grab Sarah, and then Simon would send Philip on his way to the great pie in the sky.

After it was all done, Simon Peter would come out looking like a hero for stopping Philip's crazy escapades. Simon would explain how Philip had brainwashed them. He had coerced them to participate in his scheme of Rapturing people. He would take over where Sarah had left off to prove his goodness. Matthew would give him details to help someone, and the media would be all over him after he saved a life or two. One day they may even do an exposé on him.

Except he wouldn't shun them as Sarah Roberts had. He would welcome them and explain how it all works. Eventually, he would be hired by the government or someone rich, and Simon would never want for anything in his entire life again. Looking the way he did made it even better, adding to the eccentricity of it all.

He sipped the last of his wine, thinking about how he would enjoy killing Philip.

Doubting Philip, I'm going to make you hurt bad. Real bad.

Chapter 16

Sarah slowed her pace near the dojo. The lights were still on. A brochure taped to the window advertised late-night classes on weekends.

Inside, a dozen people wearing white karate uniforms milled around, sorting through gym bags and talking.

It wasn't long before most of the attendants began to file out. She couldn't believe how perfect her timing was. She had wondered if it would be days before the dojo opened, but here she was, and the instructors were here, too. She could talk to them, express how serious things were for her, and see if they would be interested in staying a little longer tonight to teach her some basics.

After being kidnapped by Gert five years ago when her dark visions started, Sarah wanted some basic training to help survive a life of performing Vivian's bidding. She had joined the local gun club and learned how to shoot like a professional. Vivian had remained quiet during that time, only talking to her intermittently and giving her small tasks to deal with.

Caleb, her father, had known an ex-boxer who agreed to teach Sarah proper punching and how to block. Street fighting was what she wanted to learn. Survival moves for the street. But the boxer friend had limited skills in that arena.

She had tried Tae Kwon Do, but it didn't last. They focused on kicking, and Sarah was better with her hands. There was something about sticking her foot in someone's face that didn't appeal as much as jamming a fist upside their jaw.

Most of her skills were learned and then adapted to the street. When things got tense, she relied on guts and the knowledge that she wouldn't be in the mess she was in if it wasn't for Vivian. Her sister wouldn't send her into something that would see her maimed or worse.

This sense of security got her in trouble sometimes, although she couldn't shake it. The nerve to stand up to people against the odds seemed to be off-putting to most, especially because she was a young girl who weighed one-hundred-thirty pounds. Her stomach was flat and hard. The extra weight she carried was muscle from training at the gym when she was home.

She missed home. She hadn't been there in several months. The last time she'd seen her parents was when they gave her a bunch of money and sent her to Europe in search of Armond Stuart. After he was killed in Hungary, she flew back to Toronto to help Drake Bellamy, which she did. But now he was dead. Her captors, Hank and Rod, were gone. All her old enemies were dead. Just when she thought her life could go back to normal, the Rapturites showed up.

"Who the hell are the Rapturites anyway?" she mumbled to herself.

The night air cooled. She shuddered and wrapped her arms around herself. The last of the students closed the door. Inside, four men stood in a circle, talking like friends. They all appeared to be instructors.

She needed them to teach her a few tricks. If the Rapturites got close enough to touch her, she would die. Black belts probably had this kind of talent, but whatever knowledge they could impart to her within a few hours of training might save her life.

She stepped inside, taking one last look to ensure the white-powdered men weren't following her. She quietly locked the deadbolt.

The four men stopped talking and stared at her.

"What? Have I got something on my face?" Sarah asked.

No one answered.

She looked over her shoulder and wondered if they saw her lock the door. She was the visitor here, not the owner. But she had to take precautions. They would understand once she told them some of what was happening.

Floor mats covered the first half of the gym. Mirrors lined one wall. Along another, bins were filled with equipment like skipping ropes, earth balls, and yoga mats.

What kind of martial art is Shotokan?

After what she saw Waller do tonight, she was sure this was what she needed a dose of, but the foursome staring at her wasn't making her feel welcomed.

"How can we help you?" the oldest one asked.

He was cute, but he looked weathered like he'd been through something traumatic. He took an extra step to balance himself. The other three fanned out a couple of feet. All four waited to hear what she had to say. It seemed funny to Sarah that the smallest one came across as the most aggressive. He cracked his knuckles and bent his neck sideways until it cracked like he was preparing for a fight.

"I need your help," she said.

"What kind of help?"

"This may seem strange, but I need a crash course in hand-to-hand combat. Is there anything you can teach me that would enable me to keep someone's hands off me?"

"Are you in a situation where someone's hands are on you against your will?"

She realized how that sounded. "No, nothing like that. I just don't want to be touched. Well, what I mean is …"

"We have programs, classes you could join—"

"No, I can't."

"Why not?"

"No time."

"What do you mean?"

"I need to learn tonight."

The man raised his eyebrows and looked at his three instructors. Then all four of them stared back at her.

"Are you thinking you'll be attacked tonight?" he asked. "Is that why you locked my door when you entered?"

"Something like that."

He shook his head. "Nothing I can teach you in a few hours will save your life."

She was out of luck. This was a colossal waste of time. There was nothing left to say. She knew what Waller had learned took years of discipline and practice. She just thought they could teach her a couple of moves she could master in her spare time. But it was no use.

She turned to go.

"Wait."

She stopped without turning around, her back to them.

"You can learn a few things, but it would take more than one night."

She looked back over her shoulder. "I don't have much time."

"Are you in mortal danger?"

She spun around. "You could say that."

"Not any longer."

"What does that mean?"

"As long as you're in my gym, no one can touch you. You're safe here."

"Big words for someone who doesn't know me or the danger I face."

"Ah, but that's where you're wrong."

She put her hands on her hips. The speaker was attractive and well-built. She loved his confidence and his smile that wasn't a smile. The smirk was behind his eyes. He was toying with her, but she didn't know why or how much he knew.

Did he actually know her face, or was he a pig getting off on flirting with her? Maybe they had seen the news today and were already wondering how to call the police.

"Now it's your turn," she said. "Speak up. No games. What do you know?"

"I know you didn't cause that disturbance this morning at the mall."

So they did know her.

"How could you be so certain? Are you going to call the

police?" Sarah asked.

"No, and neither will my instructors."

"Why not? What's in it for you?"

"Nothing really, other than the honor of meeting the pretty, one and only Sarah Roberts." He motioned to the instructors beside him. "What are the odds that she would walk into our gym after what we said last week?"

"What did you say last week?" She felt like a fish taking the bait.

"Last year, I was in a fight for my life. I lost my sister, Joanne, to a crazy, power-hungry Brit, and then he shot me twice and broke my wrist." The man opened his white robe to show her two bullet holes in his chest. "These three men, Alex, Benjamin, and Daniel, all came to my rescue. Without them, I would be dead right now." He paused to clear his throat. "When I read about you in the paper last week and how you died in a simple car accident after all you'd done to help others, we were saddened. We need more people like you, Sarah, and if someone out there wants to hurt you, they will have to get through us first."

Stunned by his speech, weakened by a couple of near-death experiences in one day, Sarah almost dropped and lay out on the matted floor. Sheer willpower kept her standing.

"That's very kind of you, but these men—"

He waved her off. "Are they outside? Did they follow you here?"

"No."

"Then they can wait. We can start training you tonight. We'll take turns instructing you. We just ask that you give us as much time as you can. One night won't cut it. Does that work for you?"

"Yes, but why? Why help me like this? I just walked in the door."

Daniel stepped forward. "It's what we do. Self-defense. It's that simple. When we heard about you defending the weak, saving people, and getting kidnapped in their place, well, let's just say we respect that. We're more alike than you know."

She pushed on. "How are we alike?"

"We helped people that needed it last year. The bad guys are dead. Aaron got shot. His sister was killed. He even had to deal with an attempted murder charge, but it was dropped. We would love to help, but you have to be willing to accept it."

"I'm sorry about your sister," she said to Aaron. "I lost my sister to a violent murder many years ago."

"I'm sorry," Aaron said.

"How much will this cost?"

"No charge."

Aaron stepped between the three instructors and walked up to Sarah.

"My name is Aaron Stevens." He held out his hand. "Nice to meet you."

She shook his hand. His grip was firm but comforting. Her stomach tingled. He exuded an attractive strength.

"Can we continue this conversation in my office?" he asked.

Chapter 17

Simon and Philip got to the apartment door at the same time. Philip saw the eviction notice before Simon could remove it.

"Is that another eviction notice?" Philip asked.

"Nothing to worry about."

Simon unlocked the door and entered the apartment. It seemed quieter, somehow. Just this morning, they had been seven members strong. Now only three remained, with Thomas on the road. He would be in the U.S. by now. By daybreak, Dolan and possibly Esmerelda would be dead. Then Sarah's parents.

Everything he was working toward was finally coming together. If only he could get close enough to Sarah.

"We're being evicted?" Philip asked. "What are we going to do?"

"Nothing."

Philip scrunched his eyebrows together. "Nothing? How's that? We can't just ignore it."

Simon ripped the notice in half. "Actually, yes, we can. This will be all over by tomorrow, maybe the next day. We won't return to this apartment after that."

"Where will we go?" Philip asked, genuinely concerned.

"Wherever the Lord takes us."

"That's no kind of answer."

"What do you want me to say?" Simon entered the kitchen to prepare two glasses of wine and some bread. His stomach called for more, but these were the rations they had set aside when they first began.

"I don't know. I guess I just thought we'd be Raptured when this was over. I thought you said we were going to see God."

Simon chastised himself for forgetting what he had said earlier. As far as Philip was concerned, they were all dead when Sarah died.

"And I still mean it."

"Now I'm confused."

He turned and handed Philip a glass of wine. "Drink the blood of Christ first. Then we talk."

Philip sipped his wine. Simon followed suit. He collected his thoughts and said, "Let's say Matthew sends me a message tonight or tomorrow that tells us we have someone else to Rapture. Then I would continue our work in the name of the Lord. But at this point, our last communication is that we are to go home once Sarah is dealt with. So both answers are correct." Simon was proud of himself for the bullshit he spewed.

Philip shrugged and nodded. "Okay. I'm just a little rattled by seeing two more brothers killed tonight—"

"Not killed," Simon said, raising his hand to ward off the

word. "Raptured. They're at the Lord's table tonight, having a feast. If anything, feel jealousy that we aren't there with them."

Philip didn't appear comfortable with that thought. Simon could tell he was conflicted and doubting. He yearned to send him home early. He had a needle in his pocket that would have Philip out of his life for good, and all the questions went with him. But he couldn't just yet. He may need his help with Sarah. She had proved feisty. Difficult to just happen upon and take out. So, for now, Philip stayed.

But he still needed to deal with the doubt. Since there were just the two of them, he decided to let Philip in on a few secrets.

Simon set his wine on the counter.

"Would you like to see something?" Simon asked.

"Sure," Philip nodded and shrugged.

"Then set your glass down and come with me."

Philip did as he was told. Simon led him from the apartment, down the elevator, and into the basement storage facility, the building offered its tenants. It was a test of Philip's trust in Simon that he followed without hesitation or question. Simon could have taken him down to execute him, but Philip stayed close.

Maybe he had plans of his own. Maybe as Simon walked the narrow corridor between the units, Philip planned on sticking a needle in Simon. He hadn't thought of that earlier but now felt a certain kind of trepidation at the thought.

He looked over his shoulder. Philip smiled at him, staying close.

Too close.

There was a fleeting moment when Simon was sure that

Philip meant him harm. They stepped in front of unit 347, and Simon dismissed the idea. He had saved Philip's life. The man wouldn't entertain the idea of murder unless he were being attacked.

Simon fumbled with the keys trying to insert them into the lock.

"Here, I can help," Philip offered.

"It's okay. I got it."

The key slipped in. Simon turned it and opened the lock.

"What you are going to see no one knows about. This is highly secret."

Philip nodded. "I respect confidentiality."

Simon opened the door to the storage unit. Two small white fridges sat side by side on the concrete floor of the tiny storage unit.

"This is where I store all the syringes."

Philip's eyes widened, and his mouth gaped. "All of it?"

Simon met his eyes and nodded.

"But I thought you had them somewhere else," Philip said, a tone of surprise. "All this time, you've been coming down here to get more?"

"That's right. I didn't tell any of you in case you got taken alive by the authorities. I couldn't allow anyone to reveal where our stash was. But since you're the only one left, if anything happens to me, you'll need to know where they are."

"Thank you, Brother Simon, for showing me this. Thank you for your trust."

They embraced.

"It's almost over, Brother Philip."

Simon stepped out of the storage unit, waited for Philip,

and then locked the door.

"I have a spare key for you." They walked back through the corridor. "You'll keep it on you at all times in case we come back to the apartment, and the eviction has taken place."

"But, Simon, when they evict you from the apartment, they also take your storage unit. We would come down, and the lock would be cut off."

"That is true, but not our lock."

"Why not?"

"Because the unit they gave us for our apartment is sitting two rows over. It is empty and has no lock."

"Then whose unit are we using?"

"It was just an empty unit I found when roaming these halls when we moved in."

They made it to the elevator, and Simon pushed the button.

"You don't think that's risky? What if the owner decides to use it and has the locks cut off?"

"God has our back. It is his plan. Matthew told me that unit 347 will remain empty for the time we are here."

"Ah, that's good," Philip said. "That's safe then."

Simon nodded. The light was back in Philip's eyes. He didn't seem as doubtful. He had been brought in on something monumental. He had been given the proverbial key to the Rapture.

The elevator took them to their floor. Once in the apartment, they resumed drinking their wine, talked about the night's events more, and decided to retire early.

"I'm going to pray in the other room and wait for Matthew to contact me. This time we will get Sarah and send her home. Goodnight, Brother Philip."

"Goodnight, Brother Simon. I'm not tired. I think I'll go for a walk to clear my head."

"A walk?" Simon stared at him, wondered what Philip was up to, and then decided not to challenge him after regaining his faith. "Maybe that's a good idea. Then off you go. We'll see you in the morning."

Philip grabbed the keys, put his shoes on, and left.

Simon turned the apartment lights off and went onto the balcony. He only had to wait four minutes before Philip walked down the sidewalk surrounding the building.

"Good," Simon whispered from eleven floors above Philip. "I wouldn't want you up to no good. Maybe a walk is exactly what you need."

Simon went to the bedroom and closed the door. He sat in front of the altar and waited for Matthew to contact him.

Matthew did. Ten minutes later. With news of Sarah and where she would be in two days.

Matthew said he was still being blocked on some details, but he could see that Simon would have the pleasure of jamming the needle into Sarah's neck this time.

It was over. One day after tomorrow. Matthew said he saw the needle in Sarah's neck.

Thy will be done.

"Sarah Roberts, you will be dead," Simon whispered to himself, a wide, teeth-baring smile on his face.

Chapter 18

SARAH SAT IN A plush office chair on the opposite side of Aaron's desk. He had sent his three instructors home. This was a chance for Aaron and Sarah to talk and find out what she needed from him and how Aaron and his dojo could help.

"Tell me about these men in overcoats," Aaron said.

"I don't know much. They call themselves the Rapturites. Apparently, they've come to Rapture me."

"Sounds sexual."

She squinted at his playfulness. "Trust me. It's not."

"I know, I know," he said and bowed his head in an exaggerated display of shame. "Tell me more."

"They just showed up this morning at the mall. I was there as part of an exchange, which is unrelated and too long a story to tell now."

"Okay, so let me get this straight. They just walked in and started killing people?"

Sarah nodded. "What I think everyone's missing is that these people are killing for God—they really believe in the

Rapture. They can do no wrong. Even cops aren't exempt—that's how the Rapture is supposed to work, right? God takes the good ones home."

Aaron leaned back in his chair, a half-smile on his face. "Why would you say cops are *supposedly* the good guys?"

"In my experience, I haven't had a lot of faith in the authorities."

"Funny, me either."

"Cops aren't exactly well-adjusted people. They had bad childhoods, too. Some of them have seen hard shit and dealt with hard shit. That's what makes them want to be cops in the first place. Therapists are the same. They have problems, issues, and shit. We're all human at the end of the day, and we get what comes with that. I take care of myself, and everything works out. If the cops are involved, usually shit goes bad fast."

Sarah told him a little about herself and how she only really trusted Parkman over the years, who, by the way, she still had to get a hold of.

Aaron got them both a coffee as they talked. He explained what happened to his sister a year ago and how the police didn't seem to take it seriously. Once he started his own investigation, he got pulled into the Specter's sights.

"Who's the specter?" Sarah asked.

"That was the name the media gave Clive Baron, the man my friends and I ended up killing."

It was Sarah's turn to raise her eyebrows in surprise. She sat back in her chair and sipped her coffee with renewed admiration for Aaron. "Is that related to the charges you were brought up on?"

"No, that's something entirely different."

"Really?" she said as she set the coffee cup on his desk. "Do tell."

"It was a student of mine. He'd been learning martial arts to hurt people. He beat his wife and daughter, hospitalizing them. His daughter came to see me. Broke my heart. When John showed up for his next class, I made an example of him. I went too far. He was in a coma for a bit, and then when he woke, he refused to press charges against me. Everything went away."

"Wow, we really are alike."

"What else can you tell me about these guys? How do they kill so easily?"

"Needles."

"Needles?"

Sarah nodded. "They carry syringes with something in them that kills in seconds. That's why I'm here. I must learn to be fast and keep their hands off me."

"Too bad I'm not a pharmacist. I could just offer you an antidote."

"Not sure if that would work here."

"How can I help, exactly?" Aaron asked.

"Show me a couple of moves that'll keep their filthy hands off me."

Aaron grimaced. "It's not that easy."

"Why?" Sarah leaned forward and grabbed her coffee. It warmed her, calmed her, but woke her up at the same time.

"The kinds of moves you're looking for take years to learn. It involves discipline, practice, and speed. I just don't know if ..."

"I've got all that but one. I'm fast. I'm disciplined. I'll practice on my own. The only thing I don't have are years."

Silence fell between them like a dark cloak.

Aaron broke the silence. "Fine. I'll teach you what I can in the time we have. I'll focus on street techniques, keeping it simple. When you leave, you leave."

"Deal," Sarah said and stood up.

"Where are you going?" he asked.

"It's late. I'm sure you need to head home. I don't want to keep you."

"No, we start tonight. Now."

"Really?"

"Yes. We work until you're tired. In the back, there's a cot and a little fridge. Unless you have somewhere else to go, stay here. We're closed tomorrow. We can work all day."

She eyed him suspiciously. "What's in it for you?"

"What do you mean?" he asked as he stood, too.

"Nobody works for free. Where's your upside?"

"Keeping you alive."

"What?"

"I can't have you come here looking for help and then die on me. That's bad for business."

"No jokes. Be serious."

"I am, Sarah. You're too important. When you walked through that door," he pointed to the front of the gym, "I almost clapped. We read about your accomplishments, then your funeral. To see that you're alive, we can't have you die twice in one week. That would suck."

"Okay, but I won't sleep with you."

"Who said anything about sex?"

"You did."

"No, I didn't," he said as he stepped around his desk and looked down his nose at her. "Don't put words in my mouth."

"You said the Rapture sounded sexual—"

He cut her words off by putting his hand over her mouth. To ward off the attack, she leaned back over the desk so she could raise her knee. It hit him in the solar plexus. Air shot out of his mouth as she rolled away from his flailing hand. She hit the floor on all fours and, without looking to see what he was doing, pushed up and body-checked him into the wall.

Somehow, Aaron managed to wrap an arm around her shoulder. He lodged his other arm behind her head, forcing it downward. Then, before she could move away or attack again, she was bent over in a half-nelson. She leaned into it to twist out on her knees, but her feet got knocked out from under her. In seconds, she was paralyzed on her side, her legs locked in his, her neck craned to its limit, and her arms jammed upward.

"Shit," she mumbled.

He released her in one fluid motion and stood up. She turned her neck back and forth to open circulation again and then looked up at him.

Like a gentleman, he gestured to help her to her feet. She accepted and got vertical again.

"What was that for?" she asked.

"To see your level of play."

"Level of play? What the fuck is that?"

"I wanted to see if you can think on your feet."

"I guess I don't. You pinned me in seconds."

"No, you did real good."

"Huh?"

"Most people are pinned right away. You leaned away, got a knee in my gut, dropped to all fours, and tried to slam into me. Most fighters would have been injured enough to keep fighting but not win with someone like you. The only advantage I have is years of practice."

"Sucks to be you."

"Where did you learn to fight like that? It took more than instinct."

"I have a friend who taught me."

"Can I meet this friend?"

"You don't want to meet him."

"Sounds mysterious."

"I don't even want to meet him," Sarah said.

"You're confusing me."

"When this friend comes close to me, I can fight like crazy. Nothing can stop me, not even pain. I block it and deal with what I need to do."

"Ah, I think I know who your friend is."

Sarah nodded. "Death."

"Right. In a life-and-death situation, you pull out all the stops. Since this has happened to you a few times, you've developed certain skills."

"Bingo. Ultimately, I've learned to keep moving, watch for holes in my opponent's defense, and attack continuously until I repel them. If I don't, I die. Since I'm still alive, what I've done has worked."

She bounced on her feet for a second and smiled like a teenager in high school. They looked at each and smiled. Sarah giggled before she could stop it.

"Damn, I haven't giggled like a little girl in a long time."

"That's a good thing, right?"

Sarah stepped out of his office and into the main part of the gym. "I guess so, but I'm not here to be a little girl. I want to fight. You up to it?"

"Yeah," Aaron said and followed her out of his office.

Over the next few hours, he taught her three ways to get out of a bear hug, get out of a headlock, and snap a person's wrist with a simple Bic pen. To show her the wide range of Shotokan techniques, he performed two different ways to take someone's eyes out. One was a side blow with the middle finger knuckle to the temple, and the other was with both the forefinger and middle finger jabbing in above the eyeball, gouging deep, closing the fingers, and snapping out.

By three in the morning, despite wanting more, she was exhausted. She retired to the back, lay on the cot, and was asleep before Aaron locked up and left.

Her last thought was a quiet wish that Aaron wouldn't leave.

Chapter 19

Detective Waller got cleaned up by medics at the crash site. He had done his best to cordon off the area and catch the two men in overcoats but had been unsuccessful so far. The sun was rising, and he was no further ahead in finding the white-powdered men or Sarah.

Everyone had fared well in the car accident half a block up from his own. The cab driver and the pickup driver were uninjured. The couple in the cab's back seat left a statement with uniforms on duty and walked to the Xerox Tower, where they were headed when the accident happened.

From witness accounts, it looked like four men in overcoats were chasing Sarah. They had advanced from the four corners of the intersection, giving Sarah no escape. All she could do was wait for the cars to hit her or let the white-faced men grab her.

As luck would have it, two of the aggressors were dead, and Sarah was on the run. She, too, had escaped his lockdown.

Waller contacted HQ and ordered a car brought to him at the Courtyard by Marriott. It would be there in thirty minutes. That was all he needed.

He trotted down Yonge Street, up the steps, and into the hotel where Sarah had been staying. At the counter, he pulled out his badge.

"What room is Sarah Roberts staying in?"

The clerk looked like a younger version of Peewee Herman. His hair was slicked off to the side and filled with so much gel it shined. Waller could almost smell the goo.

"I can't give out information on the guests of this hotel —"

"Oh yes, you can," Waller cut in. "Sarah was almost killed tonight. I'm trying to save her life, and unless you give me her room number and a key, she will probably die. If she does, I'll arrest you as an accessory."

"Umm …" the clerk stammered.

"I also want to know what credit card she used for the room."

The clerk tried to be tough, but his face twitched and turned a shade of red. "Sir, we have a strict policy about the privacy of our guests. Without a"—he cleared his throat as he involuntarily swallowed—"warrant, I can't give you this kind of information."

"The hell you can't," Waller said as he pulled out his spare sidearm from an ankle holster and aimed it at the clerk's face. "I've been working for eighteen hours straight, and I'm fucking tired. I saw good cops get killed this morning. Sarah's connected. I need to find her, and I don't have the time to get a warrant. Cough it up, room number, a key, and how she paid for the room. Do it now before my weapon accidentally discharges."

The clerk shook in his little red jacket, his eyes wide. Waller wondered if the clerk had a hard-on for Sarah.

Is he trying to protect her?

"A man named Dolan Ryan booked the room for her, sir. I have his information right here."

The elevator opened, and a man stepped out. Waller kept his weapon in place as he walked by but used one hand to pull out his badge.

"Keep walking," he said to the guest. "Police business."

The man raised both hands, and half ran, half jogged out of the lobby.

The clerk set a piece of paper on the counter. "It's all here. That's the man who paid for the room and his home address. Sarah claimed to be his daughter, but I recognized her from the news."

Waller lowered his weapon.

"When she signed for her dinner," the clerk continued in a shaky voice, "she signed it, Sarah Roberts. But I already knew who she was."

Waller grabbed the paper and the keycard and ran for the elevators. He pushed the button and called HQ on his cell. Once he got through, he gave them Dolan's home address and asked for a cruiser to be sent to Mr. Ryan's house to pick him up. Waller needed to talk to him.

He had to learn everything about Sarah and the people that supported her if he was ever going to figure out who the white-faced men were.

Once in Sarah's hotel room, he discovered nothing out of the ordinary. In her bathroom, he saw a small spot of what looked like vomit on the side of the toilet.

"So you're human after all, eh, Sarah?"

Back in the main room, he kicked the garbage can over in frustration. There really wasn't any chance that Sarah would leave behind a clue of where she was or even a note, but he had to try.

He took the elevator back to the lobby. His cruiser sat out front, idling. He thanked the driver, who got in another car and left.

Once behind the wheel, his cell phone rang.

"Yeah?"

"Waller, it's Vince."

"What ya got?"

"We had a cruiser drive by Dolan Ryan's house."

"Good. Was he home?"

"Yeah, but … he was dead."

"Dead?" Waller almost shouted. "What the fuck? How did he die?"

"No idea. The coroner's on site. No signs of forced entry and no trauma on Ryan's body. Also, no defensive wounds. The cop knocked, and the door opened by the force of his knock. He saw the body in the front foyer."

"I bet when the ME gets done with his autopsy, he'll find where the needle was jabbed in."

"Needle?"

"Nothing. Look, we have to locate Sarah Roberts—"

"We know. Everyone's on the street watching for her."

"Whoever is after Sarah is taking out her friends, too."

"Is that this Ryan guy's connection?"

"Yeah, but who else is connected?" Waller thought out loud. "Who's gonna die next?"

"When we find Sarah, that should be the first question

we ask—"

"Wait! I got it. When we were at the mall this morning, she mentioned a name. Parker or something. Park, Parking, Parkmon, Parkman. Yeah, that's it. Find me this Parkman. I think he's a cop. He would've been up here in Toronto to attend her funeral."

"You don't mean Parkman, as in the cop friend of Sarah's who showed up here a few hours ago to help, do you?"

"Why is he there?" Waller asked, surprised as hell.

"He said he saw the attention Sarah was getting on the news and wanted to help bring her in. Get this. He said he wants to clear things up. That's not a popular thing to say when we lost so many men this morning."

"Make sure he sticks around. I'm on my way."

"Done."

Waller tossed the phone on the passenger seat, performed a U-turn, and raced south on Yonge.

It took him ten minutes to get to HQ.

"Where is he?" he asked Vince as he approached his desk.

"In the lunchroom."

Waller detoured left, dodged a couple of desks, and entered the lunchroom. It was early enough that the day shift coming on wouldn't be using it yet.

Parkman sat by himself, nursing a coffee.

"You're Parkman?" Waller asked.

He nodded and sipped his coffee around a soaked toothpick that stuck out of the side of his mouth.

"We may need your help after all."

Parkman looked up. "What happened to your face?"

"Car accident." Waller waited for a beat and then added.

"With Sarah."

"Sarah? Is she okay?"

Now you look interested.

"Yeah, she walked away from it."

Parkman smiled.

"What's funny?"

"Her luck."

"What's luck got to do with it?"

"You know that bullshit saying, 'you should see the other guy'? Well, in Sarah's case, it's true."

Waller grabbed a coffee cup, poured one for himself, and sat opposite Parkman. "What are you doing here?"

"Came to pick up my girl."

"Your girl?" Waller asked, stupefied.

"I'd say so. I think of her as the daughter I didn't have."

"Well, your girl is in a lot of trouble. Are you aware of what happened at the mall this morning?"

"Of course. And it's abundantly clear in the mall security footage that Sarah isn't to blame for what happened."

"Not directly."

"How's that?"

"Those men were obviously after her. They tried again tonight." Waller pointed at the injuries on his face. "Because of Sarah, a lot of officers are dead."

"Oh, come on, you can't lay that at her doorstep. That's like saying it's Ozzy Osbourne's fault people killed themselves after listening to his music. What's Ozzy's weapon, a pencil? All he did was write music and sing. Same with Sarah. It's not her fault that someone wants to kill her and decides to kill someone else in their pursuit of her. Doesn't wash, and you know it." Parkman shook his head, the toothpick slipping from the corner of his mouth. He watched it hit the floor, looking dejected. "Shit, got any toothpicks in this place?"

Waller ignored him. "Your American friends lied to my men and me."

"How's that?"

"This morning, they said we were apprehending a sex offender. Sarah was the bait. The perp didn't show. Instead, these guys in overcoats showed up and started killing everybody in their way."

"First, they aren't my friends. They're assholes who have hunted Sarah for too long and—"

"They're dead now."

"Good, maybe they'll leave her alone."

Waller frowned. "I just said they're dead."

"These guys don't die," Parkman said. "There's always more of them."

"How comforting."

Parkman offered a smile.

"What can you tell me about Dolan?" Waller asked.

Parkman shrugged. "He's a friend. Helped Sarah out of a pickle about five years ago. Got shot for his efforts. Got kidnapped about a year ago by the people hunting Sarah. I was there. Overall good guy. Would die for Sarah."

"He just did."

Parkman leaned over the table, his face getting close to Waller. "What?"

"He's dead. Dolan Ryan was found in the foyer of his home, dead."

Parkman leaned back and dropped his head. "Shit, Sarah's gonna be pissed."

"He rented a room for Sarah at a hotel on Yonge Street last night. I ran a check on him and had a uniform stop by to ask him if he knew where Sarah would turn up next. Found him dead."

"That's not good. Dolan had been through a lot with Sarah." Parkman shook his head.

Waller pulled out a pad and pen. "Who else would Sarah turn to? I need names. They may be in danger."

"Esmerelda Hall. She'd be next. After that, her parents. Her father, Caleb, has always been a big supporter of what she does."

Waller stopped writing. "What does she do?"

"She's an automatic writer. Her dead sister channels through Sarah to give her prophetic messages designed to help someone. Sarah does what the message says, and voila, someone is saved. The American friends you mentioned earlier have always wanted her for testing. They're probably the ones who orchestrated her funeral a few days ago. Bastards. Her parents are going to be pissed about that."

"Automatic writer, eh? Next, are you gonna tell me she reads tarot cards and looks into crystal balls? Come on. You don't believe that shit, do you?"

Parkman stared back at him, his eyes firm. He didn't respond.

"Okay," Waller said as he returned the pen to the pad. "Who else should I write down?"

"Me."

Waller met his gaze. "You?"

"Sarah and I go way back. If someone's out to kill Sarah and her known associates, then I'd be on that list."

"You're surrounded by a bunch of cops in here. I'm sure

you're safe."

"Was Sarah safe this morning at the mall surrounded by a bunch of cops?"

Waller felt physically ill.

"Sorry, that was uncalled for."

Waller ignored him. He got up from his chair, leaving his coffee untouched. He needed to plug these names into the system and get someone to check on Esmerelda and Sarah's parents.

"Wait," Parkman said.

Waller stopped at the door but didn't turn around.

"I used to know a guy."

Waller waited another moment and then turned to face Parkman.

"And?"

"Crazy dude. Had to arrest him numerous times because the courts just kept putting him back on the streets. I figured it was because he was so fucking ugly."

"What about it?"

"He suffered from something called ectodermal dysplasia. It messes with your facial features, among other things."

"Where are you going with this?" Waller asked.

"It makes the hair brittle, the finger and toenails prone to infection. The pigment of the skin can be affected, and the teeth. Man, the teeth, they come in like a vampire's. Most sufferers get dental implants. Oh, and the sweat glands are not developed because of some inactive gene or protein. These people don't sweat."

Waller started to put it together. "Are you talking about the guy on the mall footage? The ugly one?"

"Oh, say, you think I could get some toothpicks up in here?"

Waller turned to leave but stopped at the door. "Stick around a while. And I want my fucking gun back."

"Your gun?"

"Sarah stole it from my holster in last night's accident."

Parkman smiled. "I still need toothpicks."

Toothpicks? Waller asked himself. *What the fuck does he need toothpicks for?*

Chapter 20

SARAH WOKE WITH A start. For a second, she had no idea where she was or what she was doing there. The smell of fresh coffee filled the air as she swung her legs off the cot. She rubbed her face and walked into the bathroom. After using the facilities, she headed to the makeshift kitchen Aaron had set up in the back of the dojo.

"Good morning," Aaron said.

"You always this chipper in the morning?"

He turned his head sideways as if he was thinking. "Yeah, you could say that. Any day I wake up still breathing is a good day."

"Are there days you wake, and you're not breathing?"

He laughed, low and soft.

"There are a few people out there I wish would stop breathing for ten minutes," Sarah said. "That's all I ask. Ten minutes. Not much, is it?"

Aaron pivoted, two coffees in his hands. He gave her one.

"Ten minutes?" he asked. "That's all?"

She shrugged. "Yeah, why not. Would solve a lot of the world's problems if we could just get those certain people to stop breathing for ten minutes."

"We talking about the Rapturites?"

"Don't remind me."

"Sorry."

She sipped from her cup. "Mmm, this is good. You made it just right."

"Thanks. You ready for more abuse?"

"I'm starting to think that was why I was born. I'm sore as hell after yesterday."

"Sorry."

She glanced his way. "Stop saying sorry. I'm talking about the whole day. Fighting in the mall, a car accident in the evening. Then sparring with you. I feel like I fell off a motorcycle and was run over by a semi."

"Before we start, we'll do some stretches. Something of a yoga, toxin-release thing."

"I need to make a couple of phone calls first."

"Sure. Phone's over on that far wall near my office door."

"I got my own cell, thanks. They'd trace it back here."

He sipped from his cup. "You don't think they'll trace your cell?"

"Not this cell. It's not mine. Found it after the car accident last night."

"You just happened to find a cell?"

She shrugged. "Yeah."

"Oh."

They drank their coffees in silence, both looking out the dojo's front window. Sarah couldn't get what Waller had said out of her head.

We haven't got far to go. Don't worry. We'll get to the bottom of this.

What could he have meant? Where had he been taking her? Or was it an innocent comment?

"You okay?" Aaron asked.

"Yeah, why?"

"Your face. You looked angry for a second."

"Just trying to figure out what Detective Waller meant by something he said last night."

"Who's that, and what did he say?"

"He's the cop I agreed to meet with to clear up what happened at the mall. We were only together five minutes before the accident, and then I was attacked again. That was before I came here."

"What did he say?" Aaron asked as he rinsed his cup in the small sink.

"He said something about not having to go far and that we would work it out. It sounded strange. Like he was taking me to some back alley or something. Like he was going to work it out his way."

"You don't think he just meant to say that the police station wasn't far away?"

She shook her head. "No. This was different. I trust my gut on these things."

"Then it was good that you were in the accident. How long will your calls take? We should get started."

"Five minutes."

"Deal. I'll start warming up."

Sarah walked back to the cot and grabbed the cell phone from the side counter.

Two missed calls. Both were from the girl she talked to last night who had a problem with some guy—the phone's owner. She only hoped the phone hadn't been disconnected yet.

Sarah dialed Dolan's number directly. Two rings later, a man answered.

"Who is this?" Sarah asked.

"Who's this?" the man asked in a stronger voice.

"I'm looking for Dolan. Put him on."

"Can't. He's busy. But let me tell him who's calling. Your name?"

She heard a scanner or police radio in the background and then hung up.

"Shit."

Dolan was expecting me to call. What are the cops doing there?

She dialed the police department and asked to speak to Detective Waller. She was put through faster than last night.

"Waller here."

"It's Sarah."

"Sarah. Where are you?"

"Not so fast. Why are police officers at Dolan's place? He isn't part of this. I asked for his help. That was all."

"I'm sorry, Sarah."

"You're sorry—" She stopped talking and gripped the phone tight. "No. Don't tell me. No, no, no …" She dropped the phone as uncontrollable sobs shook her chest.

The flood of tears came fast. She cried, bent over on the cot. After a minute, she wiped her eyes. To Aaron's credit, he didn't disturb her.

The cell phone still ticked by the seconds of the call.

Waller hadn't hung up.

She brought the phone back to her ear again.

"What happened?" she asked.

"We don't know. It looks like he was attacked at the front door of his house. We have units on their way to Esmerelda's house and your parents' place."

"My parents? Esmerelda? Why? What do you think this is?"

"Whoever is behind this seems to want to get to the people you know."

"Why? I don't understand." Overwhelmed, Sarah wanted to crawl under the cot and not come out until next year. "How did you get Dolan's and Esmerelda's names so fast?"

"Parkman."

She lit up. "Parkman? He's here?"

"Yeah, right beside me."

"Put him on."

"But, Sarah, we have to—"

"Put him on," she shouted.

There was a moment of silence, followed by a whisper.

"Hello, Sarah."

"Oh, Parkman. I'm so glad you're safe."

"I'm glad you're safe. In fact, I'm glad you're alive."

"Yeah, the lengths some people will go to work with me, eh? Kill me first. They even had a funeral. Crazy."

"Even crazier is what's happening now. You okay, wherever you are?"

"Yeah, I'm fine for now." She peeked into the dojo where Aaron was stretching on the mats. "But I'm scared."

"Yeah, me too, Sarah. Me too."

"Don't trust Waller."

"Why?" Parkman asked. "You heard from Vivian about that?"

"No. Just something he said last night when I was in his truck."

"What?"

"Something about where he was taking me and how it wouldn't take long to work everything out. Seemed an odd thing to say to me."

"I'll keep that in mind. Listen, he wants his gun back. He's pissed about that."

"Too fucking bad. I got religious zealots after me. I need a weapon."

"I understand. He doesn't."

"Fuck him. When am I going to see you?"

"Are you safe wherever you are?"

"As far as I know, but last night those guys showed up as if they knew exactly where I would be. And Vivian said she was being blocked for some reason. I feel kinda lost."

"Listen, as long as no one knows where you are and you're safe, it's better if you stay underground until we can ID the guys on the security footage from the mall."

"You making any headway?" she asked.

"Yes. We suspect one of the guys suffers from something called ectodermal dysplasia. He's easy to spot with the big forehead—"

"You mean the ugly one."

"Yeah."

"I wondered if he did that to himself. Some people mutilate themselves and call it art."

"No, this is real. He has distinguishing features. We should be able to ID him soon."

"Is it true about Dolan?"

"Unfortunately. You gonna be okay?"

"I'll be fine. Gonna miss him, though. It's hard, Parkman, it's hard." Another wave of grief rose inside her.

"I'm going to miss him, too. Hopefully, no one else will suffer. We'll ID these guys and track them down. In the meantime, stay hidden. Call my cell if you need anything." He recited his number, and she committed it to memory.

"Parkman, let's get these bastards."

"We will, Sarah. We will."

"Have you heard about Drake yet?"

"Yes. They found a tiny hole in his neck. His body was sent away for toxicology. I'm sure they'll match it up to what's in those syringes."

Out of respect for the dead, a moment of silence followed.

"I'll buy you a shitload of toothpicks when this is over," Sarah said. "But we both have to stay alive to see you enjoy them."

She could almost hear him smile.

"All I want is a hug. I'm so glad to hear your voice. It's good to have you back in the land of the living. I hated your funeral. Do not make me go to another of your funerals. They suck."

"Yeah, I hated it too, and I wasn't even there."

Aaron stuck his head around the wall. "You coming?"

She held up one finger. "Gotta go. Be cool, Parkman. And don't let these guys touch you. They conceal those syringes in their palms."

"We know. The lab is analyzing the contents of the needles found on the two dead guys in the intersection last night."

"Good. Let me know what it is when I talk to you next."

"Will do."

"Bye, Parkman. Love you."

"Love you, too, Sarah. Stay alive."

"You too, or I'll punch your corpse so hard you'll feel it for a year on the other side."

She hung up, turned the cell phone off, and removed the battery. She couldn't allow anyone to trace her location.

Then she double-checked Waller's gun to ensure it hadn't moved under the pillow on the cot. After a couple of deep breaths, she walked to the door and leaned against the wall.

"I'm so sorry, Dolan," she whispered under her breath. "I'll pray for you. Goodbye, Drake. Vivian, if you can hear me, take care of them. I love you guys."

She wiped the tears from her face, gritted her teeth, and stepped onto the mats to fight with Aaron.

Chapter 21

In the end, he had no choice but to trust Philip. Simon agreed to let him help plan the next attack on Sarah. It would take place near Yonge and King Street, downtown Toronto. All the note said was that Sarah would be on Colborne Street around two in the afternoon. There would be a chase, but Simon and Philip would end up locking Sarah in a room and Rapturing her.

"Matthew said there would be a commotion or something," Simon said, "but he couldn't see it. Yet, Brother Philip, isn't that all we need? There is proof of the Rapture here. This is what we have been looking for all this time. It'll finally be over."

Philip nodded. "I know, Brother. It is finally coming to a close."

"We just have to wait until tomorrow afternoon. We can be Raptured after that and be home with our Lord before dinner."

Philip smiled, but Simon could tell in Philip's eyes that

he didn't have the proper faith to Rapture himself. Maybe because Simon hadn't instilled the kind of faith required to do something like that, as he wasn't going to do it either.

What Philip didn't know was whether he wanted to die or not. Simon had an extra needle planned for him. By mid-afternoon tomorrow, Simon would be the only Rapturite left, minus Brother Thomas, who was still out dealing with Sarah's parents. After Simon pleaded his case and talked of being brainwashed, he would give Thomas up. That is if Brother Thomas hadn't gotten himself killed by then.

"Come, Philip, let's have more drink. We celebrate now. It is our last day on this plane. Be joyous, be merry. We'll spend the afternoon reciting prayers for the ones left behind. We've completed our tasks as of tomorrow. It's our time to celebrate. Won't you join me?"

Philip got up off the floor as Simon's cell phone rang.

Simon answered it. "Hello?"

"It's Brother Thomas. I have good news."

He looked at Philip. "It's Brother Thomas. He brings good news." Simon turned away from Philip. "What has happened on your journey? Pray tell."

"Dolan Ryan has been Raptured."

"That's wonderful news, Brother Thomas. You have made us all proud."

"I have also Raptured the woman Esmerelda. Funny thing, though."

"What's that?" Simon asked, overjoyed that part had gone smoothly.

"It was like she knew I was coming. She opened the door and welcomed me in."

"That is funny. Maybe she was psychic," Simon said,

chuckling.

"Yeah, maybe." Thomas cleared his throat. Simon could hear the car's engine as if he was parked somewhere. "I'm sitting out front of Sarah's parents' house."

"You have done very well, Brother Thomas," Simon said, happiness spilling over into his words. "You will be rewarded. Godspeed, my brother, and see you on the other side."

"Yes, Brother Simon. Thank you for this task. You have put great trust in me. I won't let you down."

"That was why you were chosen."

"There is one other thing."

"What's that, Thomas?"

"I finished with Esmerelda and got to the Roberts's house in record time."

"Yes, Thomas. Go on."

"There wasn't a car in the driveway, but I went up to knock." His voice broke for a second. He cleared his throat. "Sorry, anyway. I knocked on the door, and no one answered." He coughed into the phone.

"Are you okay, Brother Thomas? Coming down with a cold before you go home to the Lord?" Simon smiled at Philip.

"It's just Sarah's parents weren't home."

Simon wondered why Thomas was rambling. "I know. You already said that. Wait for them to arrive. Then your task will be complete."

"I understand, Brother Simon, but someone else was home."

Simon crossed his legs and rested his elbows on his thighs. "Who was there, Thomas?" he asked, more serious now. "Did you Rapture them?"

"No, I did not Rapture them, but I want it known that I tried. The good Lord knows I tried."

Simon heard something like fear in Thomas's voice for the first time. He wondered how he had missed it before. "Who was there, Thomas? Who was at the parents' house?"

Thomas coughed and then said, "The police."

A cold feeling, like ice, wrapped around his waist, then surged through his body.

"Tell me more." Simon's face must have paled. Philip set his wine glass down and stared.

"We fought. They got the needle from me. Then they arrested me."

"That's not good. Where are you now?"

"As I said a moment before, in front of the parents' house."

"That doesn't make sense," Simon said. "If they arrested you, why would you still be there?"

"They had a communications van of some kind parked out front. I asked for my one call, and they've been so kind as to allow me to use the phone in here before they take me downtown. I'm sorry, Brother Simon, that I won't be able to complete—"

Simon hung up without another word. He stared off into space for a moment. Philip shouted something, knocking him out of his trance.

"Simon?" Philip said, snapping his fingers.

The world spun and then righted. Simon looked up at Philip.

"They have Brother Thomas," Simon said.

"They have Thomas? What does that mean? Who has

Thomas?"

"The police arrested him at Sarah's parents' house. They're onto us. He didn't get a chance to kill the parents or use the last needle on himself. But there's something else."

Philip walked over to the balcony door, stared down at the parking lot, and then glared back at Simon. "What?"

"He called me from inside the police communications vehicle at the house. He stayed on the phone," Simon broke off, staring into space. He wondered if it was all over. "He kept me on the phone long enough to trace the call." His eyes turned to Philip. "They know where we are. The police are probably on their way here now."

"Then we gotta go," Philip almost screamed. He ran across the apartment in a panic. "Let's go!"

"You're right." Simon got up off the floor. "Can you run down to the storage unit and grab as many needles as you can carry?"

"Of course."

"Then we meet at the side of the building."

"Where will we go?" Philip asked.

"Downtown Toronto, and wait for Sarah for tomorrow. I'll get our supplies and my hand cream, and then I'll meet you outside."

Philip ran out of the apartment. Simon went into the bedroom, grabbed everything they needed, and threw the salve for his hands into his pocket.

As Matthew's note said, tomorrow, they would wait for Sarah, follow her, chase her, and lock her in the room she was supposed to run to where they would Rapture her.

Simon looked forward to finally killing his enemy. Then he would take care of Philip.

In the meantime, he would enjoy his day waiting for the Rapture, preparing for chapter two in his life as an automatic writer and savior.

Nothing and no one could stop the power he and Matthew are and would become.

No one.

Chapter 22

SARAH'S MUSCLES WERE EXHAUSTED, her body heavy and hard to hold up. She felt like one large bruise. So far, Aaron had taught her over a dozen moves. Ones that flipped her opponent on their backs and other moves that knocked her opponent out cold. The problem with martial arts was that he couldn't just show her moves, and she'd learn them. He had to use her to demonstrate. Then she practiced on him. Practice was everything.

"Aaron, we're going to have to take a break. We've been at this for almost eight hours, and in that time, you've flipped me, punched me, and almost knocked me out five times." She stopped to breathe deeply as he had instructed when upside down. He held her at an odd angle, her head twisted away.

"We could stop now. Rest. Start again tomorrow."

"Yeah, okay. But, you're going to have to let go."

He released his grip, slipped his legs away, and let her down gently. At the mat, she pulled on his arms quickly, and he lost his balance. Then she twisted away, and he fell. Of course, he wouldn't just fall gracefully. He grabbed for her. She almost got away but got pulled back.

By the time they stopped, she was on her back, lying flat on the mat with Aaron on top of her. His nose rested against hers. Their eyes locked. She saw admiration, caring, and a fire in his eyes. He wanted her bad, and she could tell. She wanted him to want her. She wanted to be taken.

Slowly, he tilted his head to the side, and then his lips were on hers.

She didn't stop him.

A tingle swept through her. His lips were soft but firm, warm and moist. She allowed them passage on her lips, a place a man rarely got to go.

It felt right, comforting, but most of all, delicious. Sarah reveled in the moment as if she had finally grown up. She had matured through what she had gone through in life. She was a woman now. As a woman, she desired, yearned, wanted, and … needed.

It was easy to ignore the feelings of lust when running for her life. But under Aaron's gaze, alone on the mat, his lips on hers, she was his willful prisoner.

He slowed, parted his lips, and moved away.

"I'm sorry—"

"Don't." She cut him off. She licked her lips, taking in his essence. "There's nothing to be sorry for. Just do it again before I kick your ass."

He lowered to her lips, like he was waiting for Christmas, and kissed her again. Sarah almost cried out.

After a full minute, she pushed off the floor and spun him around until she was on top. He didn't resist. She thrust his arms wide, held his wrists down, and kissed him passionately, intimately, savoring the moment.

Then she kissed his neck. She opened his white karate uniform and kissed his chest around the bullet wounds.

"Wait," he said in a soft, bedroom voice.

Sarah paused and looked up at him. He indicated for her to get off, so she rolled off. He got to his feet and held a hand out to her.

In one fluid motion, he lifted Sarah into his strong arms. She dipped her head onto his chest as he carried her into the back.

They may have walked to the back of the dojo, but they went somewhere else, a place where fantasies were fulfilled and screams weren't pain related.

Something altogether unfamiliar for Sarah but welcomed all the same.

***

He held her for an hour as they rested in the afterglow, neither one ruining the experience with small talk. There was no talk of the future, a relationship, or if their actions were stupid.

They just held each other.

She dozed. When she woke, Aaron had gotten up and put more coffee on in the little kitchen.

"Want a cup?" he asked.

"Yeah."

When she came out of the bathroom, she saw he had set her clothes by the door.

How thoughtful.

She dressed and then walked over to the counter to get her coffee.

They sipped in silence for a few moments, their eyes averted.

"I haven't told you what happens to me when my sister works through my body."

"I have something to tell you, too," he said, shaking his head. "I have never seen that many scars on one person in my life. How are you even alive?"

"Flattering."

"I didn't mean it that way."

She laughed. "I'm teasing."

"What the hell have you been through, Sarah?"

"Hell."

"I believe you."

"How is it I'm still alive and happy?"

"Someone always has it worse."

"True."

They drank their coffees. Sarah wondered what to say about Vivian. It would take too long to tell all, but did he really need to know everything?

So she started with how Vivian had died, how it was hidden from her, and how she used to pull her hair out as a teenager to cope with the automatic writing. After their second coffee, her story brought her to the Sophia Project men and how she had just escaped their clutches yesterday morning because of the white-faced assholes who had tried to kill her—the reason she had come to Aaron's dojo.

"It never ends for you, does it?" Aaron said.

Sarah shook her head. She sat up on the counter by the sink, her second coffee half gone and now forgotten.

"But, you know, I'd do it all again."

"What?"

"Everything. I'd get kidnapped by Gert, chase Armond to Europe, and stand in the street while cars raced at me because it works. It saves lives." She kicked her feet back and forth as she looked down at them. "Vivian keeps me safe. I know there's a risk, and I've been hurt many times, but I always heal. She has never walked me into certain death. I trust her."

She looked at Aaron, who was listening intently.

"There was a time," she continued, "before I drove a stolen police car through the gates of an FLDS fundamentalist compound, that I wasn't sure if I could trust Vivian. She knew it, too. She sent me the proper message at the time to deal with where I was mentally. That's how well she knows me and how I interpret what she says. I actually feel blessed because of her."

"Wow, that's something. You go through a lot—you have it bad—but not many people would see that greener grass on the other side as you do." He lifted his fingers and dropped them one by one as he stated his points. "You get messages that send you into a den of lions. Violent criminals want to kill you. You are shot, beat up, and have bones broken, and you're feeling blessed because of that?" He dropped his hands. "Maybe that's why you were chosen because you're the only one sick enough to make that connection."

She smiled. "I like you. I like how you say what you gotta say without the worry of judgment. You're the kind of person I don't mind calling me sick."

"What are you gonna do? Beat me up?" He smiled.

She jumped off the counter as fast as she could and body-checked Aaron. He lost his balance, the wall catching him, but she was already pressed up against him.

"Maybe I will," she drawled like an Italian mobster. "Whatcha gonna do about it?"

Aaron let out a little laugh. "You are so cute. Such a tiny little girl with so much violence all wrapped up in a pretty package."

She stepped back. "Cute? I don't want to be cute."

"Too bad. You are. But that's a good thing."

"How so?" she asked.

Her hand numbed, surprising her.

"Get me paper and a pen," she snapped. "Now, damn it!"

The numbness traveled up her arm. Then she was out.

***

She woke on the floor by the sink, a pen jammed between her thumb and forefinger.

"How long have I been out?" she asked.

"Almost two minutes," Aaron said. "You wrote furiously. I asked what you were doing, but you didn't respond."

"When I'm out, I'm out. Where's the paper?"

"Here." He reached behind her arm.

"Why is it back there?" she asked. "Did I do that?"

"Just before you woke, you convulsed or something and jammed the paper behind you."

"Have you read any of it?"

"No. It's not for my eyes."

She saw the truth in his face. Then she looked at what Vivian had her write and started to cry. She curled up in a ball, hugged her legs, and wept.

Aaron tried to comfort her. He got down and wrapped his

arms around her shoulders. He waited patiently. For that, she was thankful.

She shuddered under the weight of Vivian's words and wondered what it was all for.

"Why bother?" she asked. "Sometimes this shit is really hard."

"Why bother with what?" Aaron whispered.

"Life."

Aaron stayed silent. She needed to work through it on her own. They had just met. He wouldn't and couldn't know what the right thing to say was for Sarah.

"Here. Read it."

Sarah handed him the paper.

"Who was Esmerelda?" Aaron asked.

"An old friend. Saved my life once."

"The note says she has been killed. I'm sorry." He waited a moment, then said, "It states here that it all finishes tomorrow. What does it mean by 'run into the yoga studio'?"

"I have no idea."

"You have no idea?" He sounded surprised. "I thought these notes were more specific."

Sarah wiped her eyes and looked at him. "She never details everything. Even if she did, life doesn't happen that way."

"But how can you be sure you're safe if you're supposed to just run into a yoga studio? I think running into a martial arts studio would have better odds of saving you than yoga."

"Maybe there's a certain pose I need to learn, like downward dog, that'll get these guys off my back."

"Are you being sarcastic?" Aaron asked.

"Not really. Maybe."

"Look, Sarah. This is none of my business—"

"You're right. It's not."

He looked chastised. She hadn't meant for them to argue. She shared her sister's message as a way for Aaron to see a live example of who she was. He was taking it too far. He didn't need to protect her. Actually, he couldn't.

"Sarah, you need more than a yoga studio. You need weapons. You need a Kevlar vest. How about giving this message to the cops?"

Sarah shook her head. "Aaron, please stop. If I gave the messages from my sister to the cops, they would've locked me up years ago. Some of the notes I get are about them, too. This is how I work. Sometime tomorrow afternoon, I expect the white-faced assholes to show up. When they do, I'll run. When I find the yoga studio, whatever happens after that, happens. That's it. Keep it simple. There's nothing else to it."

He watched her face for a while. Then he got up and put his shirt on.

"What happened today," he started, "was beautiful." He looked down at her. "From where I'm standing, you're a gorgeous human being with a huge heart, and I think I could grow to love that about you."

Sarah's eyes watered over.

"I'm a man of discipline. My day has a routine, whether I'm in the gym or shopping for groceries. That has brought me success in my life. What I can't live with are uncertainties, improbable things. Not knowing what's coming and just hoping for the best is too unsure for me."

"But, Aaron, it's not you. I gotta do this."

"That's where you're wrong, Sarah. What we did here, how we held each other, that's us. Each time we do that, there are more of us. Your life is so opposite and foreign to me. I'm not sure I even understand it. Murderers who want you dead are coming tomorrow, and you're supposed to run into a yoga studio." He shook his head, looking on the verge of tears himself. "That's not cool, Sarah."

"What are you saying? I shouldn't listen to my sister? The sister who has had my back for five years?"

"No, I'm saying I can't listen to her."

He stepped out of the back room and walked across the mats. From the front door, he called back, "There's food and drink in the fridge. I'll be back tomorrow by noon. We'll do this thing with me watching your back. Get some sleep."

He locked the door behind him.

She stayed on the floor where she cried, huddled into herself. There was a new hole in her where she missed Dolan and Esmerelda. And now she missed Aaron. She felt a darkness open up on the inside. With it came the knowledge that she couldn't involve Aaron.

Tomorrow, when she woke, she would leave before he showed up. She would walk the streets of Toronto, waiting, watching. When the white-faced men showed up, she would run and look for the yoga studio, just as her sister told her to.

Together, she and Vivian would end this thing so she could get on with her life.

She wondered if Aaron could be a part of her future. Then she wondered if any man could.

She curled into a tighter ball, already missing Aaron's touch.

Chapter 23

"DID YOU HAVE A good sleep?" Waller asked Parkman as he walked into the lunchroom. Parkman had a new toothpick in his mouth. "What is it with those things?" Waller asked before Parkman said anything.

Parkman ignored Waller's question. "When you picked up Sarah at her hotel, where were you taking her yesterday?"

Waller stopped moving at the cupboards, a coffee cup in his hand.

"What?"

"I asked when you picked up Sarah at her hotel, where were you taking her?"

Waller poured coffee into his cup. "I was bringing her here, to the station."

"Bullshit."

Waller spun around to face him. "What are you suggesting, Parkman?"

"Suggesting?" Parkman shook his head. "Nothing. Asking? Everything."

"There's nothing to ask and nothing to talk about. I arranged with Sarah to bring her in so we could take her statement. I need to find out who killed my officers. Someone has to pay. We've got cops coming from all over North America for the funerals. I will have someone in custody before those officers arrive."

"What arrangement did you make with Sarah? No one I've talked to at HQ knew you were picking her up. I saw the security footage from the mall. It was clear to me that Sarah was running for her life as much as your officers. The murderers were easy to see. Why smear Sarah's name with the media as a person of interest, like she's a suspect when she's done nothing wrong?"

A surge of heat rose above Waller's neck. He wondered how red his face was getting.

"I'll agree that it looks like they were after her. Anyone watching the footage would've seen that."

"Right. So why is she a suspect?" Parkman asked.

"I have to do whatever I can to get answers. Sarah Roberts is a person of interest. We still don't have her statement, and now she has committed another offense by stealing my weapon."

"So getting the whole city after her was the answer? And, by your own admission, you were knocked out when your gun went missing. No one can verify who took your weapon. It could've been one of the men who helped you out of your vehicle."

"You're unbelievable." Waller walked to the table and looked down at Parkman. "If those white-faced guys were after her, she would know why. She was our best lead to finding them. My men want answers. Someone has to pay for what happened to the officers who were only supposed to handle the exchange of a sex offender. Do I have to remind you that we were there under false pretenses? We were unprepared. Sarah Roberts is a hero among many for her ability to help people. Why didn't she help my men?"

"We'll have to ask her. But, remember, she's not God. She's not all-knowing. And about your men, I, of all people, understand that. We do need answers."

Waller moved away from Parkman, afraid he might jam the toothpick into his mouth. "So why the cross-examination here? Why piss in my coffee this morning?" Waller took his first sip of coffee by the door.

"Because something isn't adding up, and until it does, I can't trust Sarah's safety with you or any of your officers."

"I saw those guys last night. We've nabbed the one who calls himself Brother Thomas, and we had men raid Brother Simon's apartment last night, where we just missed them. We're onto them. It's only a matter of time before we capture 'em."

Parkman raised his nose to smell the air. "Can you smell that?" he asked.

"No, what?"

"Bullshit. I smell bullshit."

"Fuck you, Parkman. You can leave anytime. Go back to the States where you belong." Waller stepped through the door.

"Yeah, sure, okay. Since I'm the only one Sarah trusts, that would be the right move. I'll just tell her when she calls in again that you ordered me out. That'll endear her to you."

Waller stopped. He stepped back through the door. "What is up with you? Stick around then. I don't fucking care. Just stay out of my way."

"Where were you taking her, Detective Waller? Tell me, and we'll continue working together. Lie to me, and I will keep Sarah from you. You'll never see her or talk to her. When this is over, she'll turn up in the States somewhere, a long way from here. Come on, you've read about her exploits. You don't think she can just disappear? Her sister can outwit any of you."

Waller thought about it for a moment. He checked behind him, saw no one was coming, and stepped back into the lunchroom. He sat at one of the tables and placed his coffee in front of him.

He met Parkman's gaze. "We almost nailed the trace of the phone Sarah was using when she called you."

Parkman nodded.

"And we called in a specialist to educate us on the condition of the ugly one."

Parkman nodded again. "You're a good cop with a good record. I expect nothing less. You'll cover all the bases. What's that got to do with Sarah?"

Waller lowered his head but didn't take his eyes off Parkman. "I didn't tell you everything."

"I'm listening."

"When Hank Frommer approached us, he had an official from his embassy in Toronto coordinate the meet in the Allandale Centre. We were informed that the trade was Sarah for a man named Rod Howley."

"I'm aware of this. And Rod was supposedly a sex offender, yada yada. None of it's true. But go on."

"The file we were given informed us on who Sarah was, too."

Parkman leaned closer. "And ..."

"It was my team going in there. The file said that if anything went wrong, it was because Sarah had set it up."

"How could that be?" Parkman asked with obvious disbelief. "She was their virtual prisoner. They staged her death and brought her parents up for the funeral."

Waller shook his head. "We pulled the DNA from the car accident. I called her parents."

"You?"

Waller nodded. "Then the U.S. government guys call and say she faked her death. It's all part of the international immigration scam that she busted back in Hungary and Italy —"

"What? You have got to be kidding."

Waller sipped his coffee. "Let me finish. We were told." He stopped to correct himself. "I was told that Sarah was wanted on murder charges, a list of other indictable offenses, and such. We were informed that she hates cops and wanted to see them executed for what happened to her sister. Hank Frommer personally sat down with me and told me if the Allandale Centre exchange goes wrong, then look at Sarah. She orchestrated the whole thing. She even threatened Hank's wife. He had the notes in Sarah's handwriting to prove it." Waller took a large swallow of his coffee and then put the cup down. "Can you see why we're all a little pissed at Sarah? She did this. Her actions, whatever they were, set this in motion, and now I have a lot of dead cops and no one in custody."

"That whole story is a fabrication. Sarah was in custody herself. Hank kidnapped her. Those notes are what Sarah does. She channels her sister—"

Waller stood abruptly. "Yeah, right, fortune-telling again. Next, you're going to tell me there are angels and a God." Waller shook his head. "No, Parkman. You're talking to an atheist. There is nothing beyond this shit piece of hell we call earth. There is no God and no afterlife. No one channels shit from some long-lost sister." He was shouting now. "Once everyone gets that and stops making Sarah into some national fucking psychic celebrity, everything will get back to normal."

Parkman stood. "You are the wrong cop to be working this case. Arrange for someone else to go after Sarah Roberts. Transfer out."

Waller surprised himself by throwing his coffee cup across the lunchroom. It hit the wall a foot above the sink and shattered.

"Why is that?" he shouted, stepped closer to Parkman, and looked down as he towered at least a foot over him. "Tell me. Because she's a little girl running around my city causing accidents and getting my officers killed?"

Parkman didn't back away. He stepped closer until his chest touched Waller's.

"No. Because for you it's personal. You've already got it in your head that she's guilty. She hates cops, and you're the reason. Cops like you fuck it up for the rest of us. If you get in her way, the accident last night will seem like a vacation to what she will plan for you."

"Are you threatening a fellow officer?"

"Vivian listens. Vivian plans. Sarah executes. Nothing touches or gets near Sarah without Vivian's okay. That's why, even after you got her last night, you lost her. Re-examining that scenario, all I see was a convenient way for Vivian to give Sarah a weapon and embarrass you in the process."

Outside the lunchroom door, officers gathered, curious about the shouting and the coffee cup shattering. Waller pointed at them. "Watch yourself, Parkman. One more word, and I'll have my men arrest you. Then you won't be any help to your precious Sarah."

"Arrest me on what charge?"

"Uttering death threats to a peace officer. I will hold you for twenty-four hours." He smiled. "I'm sure this thing will be over by then."

"I'm so sick of all the shit Sarah has to go through when all she wants to do is help people. Why does she always have to be the victim?" He shook his head and looked down at the floor. "Fuck you, Waller, fuck you."

Parkman sat down in the same seat he'd occupied a moment before. Waller briefly contemplated arresting him, keeping him out of the loop, but didn't want to deal with the paperwork when he needed to focus on nailing Sarah Roberts and her white-faced friends.

"Stay out of my way, Parkman, or this ends badly for you and Sarah. Don't leave this building. If I see you downtown or anywhere near Sarah until this is over, I'll consider you a hostile, colluding with a suspect. Things'll go south fast."

Waller pushed past the onlookers, ran downstairs, and left the building. He got on his cell phone and organized uniforms to double up the foot patrol in the Yonge, Jarvis, and Church Street areas. He wanted everyone on the lookout for Sarah. Wherever she was, the white-faced goons were, too. He felt lucky. Today he would get her, and he wouldn't count on any celestial help.

Sarah Roberts would pay for what she did to his platoon,

and he was just the man to exact that revenge.

Chapter 24

Sarah checked the time and saw that it was almost noon. She must have been exhausted to have slept that long. Aaron would be back anytime soon, and she didn't want to be there when he returned.

She threw water on her face and made up the cot. She grabbed Waller's gun, the cell phone with the cracked screen, and left the dojo through the back door as it locked behind her.

Goodbye, Aaron.

They had a beautiful time together, but she didn't need a protector. Just because they slept together once didn't automatically slot him in the role of protector. She had to fight her own battles. She knew it was more about protecting him, though. She couldn't allow him to get close or be close because he could get hurt, and she didn't want that on her conscience. The Rapturites didn't care who got in their way.

She walked south on Jarvis, focusing on her surroundings, watching for the white-faced thugs or a yoga studio. It was like looking for the exit signs in an airplane so that if something went wrong, she would know which way to run. As soon as she saw a Rapturite, she didn't want to have to find a yoga studio. It might be too late.

She contemplated putting the cell phone battery back in but worried it would give her position away if they were still trying to track her. It had a purpose to serve when she was ready.

Cars whizzed by, and pedestrians crowded the street. She walked around the people, hoping she remembered some of the moves Aaron had taught her when the time came. It was the easy moves that came to mind. Snapping out of a wrist grab or twisting out of a two-handed grab around the collar. She thought she'd be able to get out of a headlock much easier, too. But none of that mattered if a needle entered her when she wasn't looking.

Panic pitted her stomach, and her legs were weak. How could she think that she could take these guys on by herself? All they had to do was get close enough to touch her, and she would die.

"This is crazy," she whispered.

She looked around, wondering if someone had heard her, then realized that she would probably fit right in with the eccentric people of the big city. She had passed street preachers, men with placards announcing the end of times, and bums talking to themselves. They had interesting conversations, but Sarah never stuck around long enough to hear everything.

Behind her, a young man in a baseball cap ducked behind a car. She stopped and stared, waiting for him to get to his feet.

Am I being followed?

The afternoon humidity added to the summer heat. It was probably only eighty-five degrees Fahrenheit, but it felt ninety-five. Sweat beaded on her forehead, her hands clammy.

She watched, but the young man didn't reappear. Waller's gun in her waistband comforted her as she approached the car. Two women in their mid-twenties walked by just as she reached the parked car. She hopped around the edge, but the area was empty.

What the hell? I saw him.

She scanned the area, but he was gone. Across the street, she thought she saw a man watching her through a bookstore window. She stared hard, but the man put something back on the shelf and walked away.

Am I losing my mind? Is the pressure getting to me?

She walked south on Jarvis again. She turned right at the next block, then left on Church Street. It was after lunch, and she hadn't eaten yet. She contemplated what she would eat or if she would see the Rapturites before she had the chance. Maybe she should've eaten before she left Aaron's dojo, even if she'd grabbed something to leave with. Thinking about the dojo brought her back to Aaron. She had tried to keep him out of her mind. Missing him, yearning for him, could get her killed. She needed to stay focused and watch for the bad guys, but Aaron's face pulled her back to him.

Maybe one day, maybe.

She had to finish this. She had to lead her followers into a yoga studio and let whatever was supposed to happen, happen. Then she would get on with her life. She would travel to the States and go to Dolan's and Esmerelda's funerals. She would visit her parents, and maybe it was time to go on the road. She would buy a motorcycle and travel. Drive from border to border, see the country, and help people anonymously, just like she did in the beginning. Maybe she should start wearing her bandanna again.

And maybe she should write a book about her adventures. She could write a memoir or a novel. Or a series of novels.

But who would want to read about my life?

She slowed by a coffee shop to look in the reflection of the glass. People moved up and down the street. Cars went by. She looked for anyone not moving, watching her.

Nothing.

A cop car cruised by slowly. She thought the driver was watching her. She stared at the window, pretending to read the shop's menu. The cruiser passed, and she turned south again.

She watched for a yoga studio.

This is ridiculous. I feel so lost.

"Yoga studio, Vivian? Really?"

She kept walking, sure the white-faced assholes were close by.

***

Aaron texted Alex, telling him to give her more room. She almost made him by the car. Even though Sarah had briefly met Alex, Daniel, and Benjamin the night she walked into the dojo, it didn't mean she wouldn't recognize them if they got too close.

Aaron had arranged for his three instructors to meet him

a block down from the dojo at eight that morning. He told them what Sarah was up against and that someone had killed two of her friends in the States. She was distraught and supposed to deal with these guys today. They had argued about her running into a yoga studio instead of a karate dojo or even a police station. But Sarah was headstrong, determined to follow her note exactly.

Aaron was headstrong, too. After they had shared something together that Aaron hadn't shared with anyone in many years, he was determined to watch her back today, whether she liked it or not. He had almost had a fling with a girl named Julie, a waitress from a local club in Toronto, a year ago after his sister died, but it had proved too painful. Painful because of the grief he had to deal with at the loss of his sister. She had worked at the same club as Julie. It was also painful physically. He was in physiotherapy at the time. Julie had drifted away, and Aaron had been officially single for the last nine months.

He wasn't about to let Sarah get hurt or worse.

Daniel texted that he had her going south on Church Street. Benjamin texted a moment later that he would relieve Daniel at the next corner. Alex said he would stay far back to avoid being seen. Aaron had to stay back the farthest, although she almost saw him in that bookstore. For a second, he was sure she saw right through his flimsy disguise of a stupid fake seventies mustache. After putting the book back on the shelf and turning to walk away, Alex texted him that Sarah had moved on.

He ran down Jarvis to get a couple of blocks ahead of Sarah's position and find a restaurant or coffee shop to hide in until she passed by.

Police were everywhere, but he brushed it off. Now that he was looking for cops, they were on every corner. They were probably always there, but he'd never noticed them.

Or maybe they knew what was going to happen today. Would Sarah have called them for backup?

Today was a big day for Sarah. Aaron would be there when she needed him the most.

Nobody hurts one of his students. Especially not one he has fallen for.

Chapter 25

Last night, Simon and Philip rented a room in a small hostel-like residence in downtown Toronto. When Simon went out for two coffees that morning, he had noticed numerous police foot patrols. It was a bad day to hunt Sarah downtown Toronto, but Matthew's note had been specific. Simon would see Sarah on Colborne Street near Church Street during the early afternoon. They were to follow her. Once inside the building, wherever it was, Sarah would take them, and Simon would get his chance to plunge his needle into her flesh and end her human existence.

Matthew had said he saw the needle in Sarah's neck. Matthew had never been wrong since he had started sending Simon messages. There was no doubt that Sarah would be Raptured today.

They just had to wait. She would show up any time. Simon and Philip sat on the bumper of a car in a city parking lot that looked out on Church Street and the length of Colborne. It was a great spot to keep an eye on the area without raising any eyebrows.

They had counted six patrols of police officers doubled up and walking the length of the street. Two of them had talked into their radios. They had to have been tipped off somehow, but it didn't matter to Simon. When this was all over, he would be the hero. Once everyone saw what he could do, they would grow to love him. Philip would be dead and could never testify against him.

He only had to deal with Thomas. But he figured he could. Matthew would help with that. Maybe he would claim he was brainwashed and Thomas was behind the whole thing. With the current state of the Canadian court system and laws, they wouldn't get more than a couple of years in jail if everything went against them. Then he would start his new life as the savior.

"I'm happy you decided not to use the rice powder," Philip said.

"We would stand out too much."

"After we're done with Sarah, we're heading home anyway." Philip fiddled with his fingers. "Do you think it'll hurt when we die?"

Simon turned to him. "We're already dead, Brother Philip."

"How so?"

"The real death is coming here. We live on the other side. We die when we come here. We wake up—alive—when we go home. That little indent under your nose, just above your lips, is where the angel touched you before you were born on earth." He demonstrated this by touching his own upper lip. "They touched you here and said, 'Speak not what you know.' That's how ninety-nine percent of us just go about our day-to-day lives, not realizing or thinking about the fact that we're only here for a short time while we wait to head home and begin living again. Except us, of course."

"Except us?" Philip asked.

"Yeah, us. We know. Matthew has told us. We're the privileged ones. We're on a mission from God. Rapturing people has been an honor, and all we have left to do is Sarah. Once we do, Sarah, we're done and can finally go home."

He reached into his pocket and pulled out the salve. The cracks in his fingers were hurting again. After rubbing a liberal amount on, he shoved the salve away and stepped out of the shadows to get a better look up and down the street.

"How many needles do you have on you?" Simon asked.

"Three."

"I remember asking you to run down to the storage unit and grab as many as you could carry."

"I know, but once Sarah's gone, we're done, so I didn't think we'd need more than three each. One for her, one each for us, and a couple of spare in case we run into trouble again."

Simon wanted to turn around and smash a couple of needles into Philip's eyes but controlled himself. He may still need him.

Then he saw her.

Sarah Roberts walked south on Church Street as if she didn't have a care in the world. Every time Matthew's prophecies came true, he was still mystified.

"I got her," he said to Philip.

"Where?" Philip moved close.

"Walking right there, about a hundred yards from us."

"Okay, good. Let's end this."

"We will, but we have to wait."

"For what?" Philip asked.

"For her to pass us. Then we follow her. We'll do it when we're alone somewhere. Fewer witnesses."

"What do witnesses matter if we're going to Rapture ourselves as soon as she's gone?"

"Good question, Brother Philip. Just trust me. We do it my way."

Philip shrugged.

They stepped back to remain concealed behind the vehicles in the parking lot.

"Check my hair and eyes," Simon said. "I'm good?"

"Yeah. Me too?"

"Yeah."

They both checked the street again. Sarah stopped at the corner of another parking lot across the street and pretended to tie her shoes, but Simon could tell she was watching her back.

Then she moved close to a vagrant sitting on the side of the street with a German shepherd wrapped in a blanket. She pulled something out of her pocket, fiddled with it, and then held it in front of her. It looked like she was talking into it. After a moment, she reached down and gave it to the vagrant.

Then she started across a parking lot.

"Come on, let's go," Simon said. "It's time Sarah Roberts died."

Chapter 26

Parkman sat in the lunchroom as long as he could. He'd called Sarah's parents and assured them Sarah was fine and that he would probably see her later in the day. He discovered that Dolan and Esmerelda would be buried in the same cemetery in three days. He told Sarah's parents that he would do what he could to be there and bring Sarah, if at all possible.

Then he called his HQ to get all the information he could on whatever the ugly suspect suffered from. While he waited for a return call from a medical professional that owed him a favor, he went into the video room and got the technician to bring up the mall security tapes to see if he had missed anything.

The footage mostly covered the shoppers' mass movement as they tried to get out. Parkman watched as panic broke out. He slowed the images racing across the screen to watch for Sarah. After she moved away from Hank, she ran for the sporting goods store.

Good thinking, Sarah. Weapons are in there.

The glass broke beside her. She dove to the floor and then, on her belly, crawled into the store.

How did the glass break? Random gunfire?

Parkman asked the tech to mark the time to the second on the camera that showed the glass breaking and then set up the other tapes to see if he could catch what everyone else was doing at that second.

It took two different cameras before he saw Detective Waller hiding inside a food court booth. He got the footage fast-forwarded until seconds before the glass broke in the sporting goods store.

He leaned forward as the camera inched along, watching Waller's every move. At two seconds away, Waller seemed to search the area or watch something. At one second, Waller raised his weapon and aimed across the food court. At the exact second the glass broke, a flash appeared at the tip of Waller's weapon.

"Holy shit!" Parkman shouted as he dropped back in his chair. "Waller shot at Sarah. He tried to kill her."

He told the technician to print all the footage's images at that second and stick them in a manila envelope for him. He would be back later to pick it up.

Then Parkman ran out of the building, heading for his rental car. Waller was after Sarah, and they were both downtown somewhere. He was new to Toronto, but he knew Waller was focused on the area where he lost Sarah last night. He would drive his rental to Yonge Street and then call Waller to find out where he was. Waller would tell him, too, once he knew what Parkman had discovered.

The attempted murder of an American citizen and the

security footage at the mall would verify it.

Waller was finished.

Parkman smiled.

Chapter 27

SARAH SAW HIS FOREHEAD first. He had leaned out of a parking garage across the street. A moment later, she saw a yoga studio on the second floor of a building on the other side of the parking lot in front of her.

She stopped in front of a bum sitting on the sidewalk, her back to the Rapturites. The cell phone battery slipped inside the back of the phone easily. She powered it up and called Detective Waller's number. She put the phone on speaker and told him she was downtown and about to be followed by two of the white-faced guys.

"Where are you?" he asked in his husky, heavy voice.

"I don't know exactly. I'm not from this area. I think I'm on Church Street. I was on Jarvis. But I'll leave the battery in the cell. Triangulate its signal. You'll find me across the street in the yoga studio. But hurry. I don't want to use your gun on these guys, and I don't want to be touched by them."

"I'm five minutes away. I have men closer."

"Find the phone; you find me."

"I'll call it in on my way over."

"Bye, Waller. Can't talk anymore, but I won't turn the phone off."

Sarah bent and proffered the cell phone to the bum.

"Here, take this."

"For me?" he asked.

"Yeah. Just don't turn it off for at least five minutes. Can you do that?"

"Why?" he asked. "Am I in trouble?"

She needed to go and had no idea what kind of explanation a street bum would need. She tried a version of the truth.

"There are men with white faces following me so they can Rapture me. This cell phone signal is beaming up to the cell towers, telling the people who are going to stop the fight for Armageddon from happening. Beings from the other side are involved. This is important to the future lives of many. Can you handle this?"

His eyes widened. He nodded slowly, looking at the phone as if it were a bar of gold.

"I'll protect it," he said as she moved away.

She dodged through cars and vans in the full parking lot, hurrying to the far corner where she could cross the street and enter the yoga studio.

She had no idea what would happen next. All she had was Vivian's note and a hope that surpassed her instinct of self-preservation.

She would live if she did exactly what Vivian told her to do.

At least she hoped so.

****

Simon and Philip stepped from the garage into the afternoon sun. The heat hit Simon right away. He wavered on his feet, but it didn't matter. His target was close. They were almost done. Nothing would get in his way this time. Matthew had told him so.

They ran across the street when there was a break in traffic and approached the vagrant Sarah had stopped in front of.

He took a quick look to see where Sarah was going and saw her enter the front doors of a yoga studio between a men's fitting store and a restaurant.

He turned back to the vagrant.

"What did that woman give you?" he asked.

"Nothing," the man said as he moved a hand along his dog's back.

"Don't lie to us. We saw her give you something." Then he had a thought. "It's a matter of national security."

"What?" the man said. "She didn't say anything about that. This cell phone is to help track the white-faced guys—"

Simon reached down and snatched the phone out of the man's hand.

"Hey!" the vagrant yelled. "You can't do that."

Simon turned toward the traffic. A long semi-flatbed was passing them. He tossed the phone onto the back of the truck.

"Sorry. Misunderstanding. You can have your phone back if you can get it."

Simon took off after Sarah with Philip on his heels. The vagrant shouted about end times as Simon and Philip ran through the parking lot Sarah had just traversed.

He has no idea how right he is.

***

Aaron got the text from Benjamin that Sarah had stopped to talk to a bum on the sidewalk. She handed him something and took off through a parking lot. He couldn't handle it anymore and called him.

"Yeah?" Benjamin said as he answered his phone.

"Where is she now?"

"No idea."

"What? How could you have no idea? You were the closest to her."

"She stopped and talked to this bum. Then she gave him something and ran away—"

"Where are you exactly?"

"Near the corner of Church Street and Colborne."

"I'm on my way, but tell me what else happened."

"I stayed back. About two blocks away when she stopped. After handing the bum something, she ran off to the right through a parking lot. I lost sight of her but thought I'd pick her up again when I got to the bum."

"And?"

"When I started running, two guys ran across the street and talked to the same bum."

"What? Those are probably the guys that are after her."

"One of them grabbed what looked like a cell phone from the bum and tossed it onto a truck going by. Then they ran in the same direction Sarah had gone."

Aaron was running now, the wind making it hard to hear on the phone.

"What else?" he shouted.

"When I got to the corner, the two guys that stopped at the bum were gone, too."

"I see you. I'm a block up. Text Alex and Daniel to join us."

Aaron ran the rest of the block, passing two sets of foot patrol cops on the way, but neither paid any attention.

He got to Benjamin and put his hands on his knees to catch his breath. Seconds later, Alex and Daniel joined them.

"What do we do?" Benjamin asked.

"We find Sarah," Aaron said.

"I know. But how?"

Daniel stepped inside their circle. "How about calling the police? There seem to be quite a few down here today. If it's the same guys from the mall massacre, then Sarah's probably in more trouble than we can help her with."

Aaron frowned.

"Maybe he's right," Benjamin said. "Did you read what the witnesses said? All those guys had to do was touch someone, and they died."

"We can't call the cops," Aaron said between breaths.

"I hope this isn't a recurrence of last year," Benjamin said. "Doing it all on your own shit."

Aaron frowned at him. "No. Sarah talked to the cops in the back of the dojo. I overheard her talking to a cop named Parkman. She said she trusted him. When talking to Parkman, she told him to watch out for Waller."

"Who is this Waller guy?" Alex asked.

"He's the guy all over the news the last few days looking for Sarah, claiming she had something to do with the killings at the Allandale Centre. At least that's how it sounds."

"Okay, then it's solved," Daniel said. "We don't call the cops. We call this Parkman dude."

Aaron told his three-man team to spread out and look around the area for any sign of Sarah or the two thugs as he pulled out his cell phone and dialed the police, hoping they could transfer him to a cop named Parkman.

Then he remembered something else Sarah had said. She would buy Parkman a box of toothpicks when this was all over.

The police operator picked up.

"Hello," Aaron said. "I'm looking for a cop by the name of Parkman who is up from America and may be assisting on a case with Detective Waller. He's the one who loves toothpicks. It's regarding Sarah Roberts."

Chapter 28

PARKMAN'S PHONE BUZZED IN his pocket.

"Yeah?"

"Hi, it's dispatch. I got a guy on the phone who said he has information on Sarah Roberts, and he said he would only talk to you."

"Put him through." Parkman exited the Gardiner Expressway and started north on Yonge Street. There was a click, silence, and then an open line with traffic going by in the background.

"Hello, Parkman?"

"Yeah, you got him."

"How do I know it's you?"

"Who is this?"

"No, it doesn't work like that. Figure out a way to prove that you're Parkman, Sarah's friend; then I'll tell you why I called."

"You asked for Parkman, right?"

"Yeah."

"They put you through to me. That's not good enough for you?"

"No."

"Why not?"

"Sarah said she couldn't trust the cops. I have a history of the same thing. I don't care who the fuck they put me through to. All I want to know is if you're Parkman. If you are, Sarah's in trouble and needs your help."

"I know she's in trouble. That's why I'm downtown Toronto driving around, trying to find her."

"Along with a thousand other cops."

"I'm seeing that," Parkman said as a second pair of officers in uniform walked by his car.

"You're still not saying anything to prove you're Parkman."

"What do you want me to say? Shit, just tell me what's going on."

"No deal. I'm hanging up unless you talk fast."

"Okay, hold up. I've known Sarah since she got away from her kidnapper about four or five years ago. She has friends who just died." Parkman choked up for a second and then continued. He talked fast, rambling on about everything from Sarah's parents to Europe and his helping her in Budapest. He finished with his love of toothpicks and her always teasing him about them.

"That'll work," the caller said. "I'm Aaron Stevens. A friend."

"How do you know what I said was the truth?"

"No time for that, Parkman. Sarah's in trouble."

"Geez, sorry."

"We followed her—"

"Who followed her?"

"Just listen. No, wait, where are you?"

Parkman strained to see the sign coming up. "I'm on Yonge and … King Street."

"Turn right on King."

"Why?"

"I'm directing you to where we are."

"Good timing. I was just about to go through this intersection."

"When you hit Church Street, turn right again. You'll see us on the side of the street before Colborne. We'll watch for you. What are you driving?"

"A red Chrysler 300."

"Okay. You're about a minute away."

Parkman ended the call and hit the gas. He turned at Church and saw them right away. He parked in the lot beside them, got out, locked the car, checked that his weapon was secure, and stepped up to the foursome.

"You the one who called?"

"Yeah, Aaron," he held out his hand. "Alex, Daniel, and Benjamin."

Each man shook.

"Now," Parkman said. "Start from the beginning."

Aaron told him about Sarah training with him in the back of the dojo and how she got a message from her sister. He covered everything, right up until his decision to follow her and protect her with the help of his trusted instructors. But they lost her at this exact spot.

"What did the note say? That's how you find Sarah."

"I didn't memorize it. It told her that Esmerelda was dead. The rest was something about her running into a yoga studio. We argued a little about that. I said why not run into a dojo or a police station. Why a yoga studio?"

Parkman did a full scan of the area and stopped when he saw a yoga studio on the other side of the parking lot.

"How long ago did you lose her?" he said as he walked away.

"At least ten minutes now. Maybe fifteen."

"And you didn't think to try the yoga studio over there."

"Oh shit, didn't see it."

All five men sprinted across the parking lot.

Chapter 29

Sarah ran through the front doors of the building and stopped to see how close the two Rapturites were. They had paused to talk to the vagrant on the sidewalk. She wondered if they'd found the cell phone, turned it off, or destroyed it.

She took the stairs two at a time and entered the front room of the yoga studio. There was a main desk where a woman sat and two leather chairs in opposing corners.

"Can I help you?" the woman asked.

"Yes. How many people are here today?"

"Excuse me?"

Sarah ran to the window and looked down at the street. The two goons had finished talking with the bum and started across the parking lot toward her.

Options disappeared. Her hand gripped Waller's gun as she returned to the woman at the main desk. She pulled out the weapon and aimed it at the woman.

"I said, how many people are here?"

The woman screamed, put her hands to her face, and

pushed back on her swivel chair, her wide eyes not leaving the weapon.

"Focus, woman. Where are all the people?" Sarah asked. "In a class?"

The woman nodded, her hair falling out of her loose bun.

"Is there another stairwell out of here?"

She nodded again.

Sarah grabbed her arm, lifted her off the chair, and pulled her through the double doors that led into the studio. She locked them behind her, and a wave of heat hit her.

"Why is it so hot in here? Air conditioner broken?"

"Bikram," the woman mumbled.

"What? Speak clearly."

"Bikram yoga."

She pushed the woman toward the students who sat cross-legged on the floor in rows, staring at her, sweat dripping.

"Everyone up," Sarah yelled. "Now."

The yoga students rose as one without using their hands.

"If you want to live, leave through the back entrance of the building. There are two men coming in the front right now that caused the killings at the mall downtown. You will die in a yoga studio massacre if you're caught here."

They didn't hesitate. The students ran for the back corner as a unit, leaving their mats behind. Some whimpered, and one woman panicked near hysterics. Sarah followed them to the rear and spoke to the receptionist.

"What's Bikram yoga?"

"Hot yoga."

Sarah grabbed her shoulder and held her a moment longer. "Explain it."

"We do twenty-six poses over ninety minutes at over one hundred degrees."

Everyone had cleared the stairs in front of them.

"Interesting." But she was out of time for chatting. "Go down with your friends and call the police."

"You want me to call the—"

"Yes. Ask for Detective Waller. Tell him where we are. I'm Sarah Roberts."

"You're Sarah Roberts ..." the woman lunged as Sarah checked over her shoulder to see if the white-faced goons had made it to the yoga studio door yet.

The gun flew from her hands, hit the top of the stairwell, and clanged over the railing, heading to the bottom. Sarah reacted, but it was too late. She shoved the woman hard, closed and slammed the door, locking it from the inside.

"Shit," she mumbled. "Now what?"

She had nothing to defend herself with. The temperature in the room seemed to increase with each passing second.

Why the hell would people willingly do yoga at this temperature?

Maybe it was a good thing she didn't have the gun. It would be too tempting to just shoot the idiots when they busted through the door. Vivian had told her to not shoot them.

Bring it on, then. I'll play the victim.

Someone tried the doorknob across the room. Sarah found a chair, moved it to the center of the room, and sat down to wait.

The police were on their way. She had them track her. Any minute Waller would barge in and arrest her pursuers. In the meantime, she would fight them off with whatever street fighting she knew, combined with what Aaron had taught her.

Someone banged into the door. They were trying to break the door down.

Five seconds later, after two more attempts, the door gave.

The two men stepped into the room, a needle in each of their hands.

"Hello, Sarah. It's time. The Rapture is upon us."

***

Detective Waller screamed into his radio as he came up behind a flatbed truck with his lights flashing and siren wailing.

"This can't be Sarah. She wouldn't be in a fucking truck."

When the truck stopped at a red light, Waller got out of his cruiser and ran alongside. He pulled his sidearm as he got to the passenger side and jumped up to look inside.

The driver started in his seat at the sight of the weapon.

Waller shouted, "We thought you had somebody with you."

The driver shook his head, wide-eyed. "Nobody's here."

Waller jumped down, but not before seeing a cell phone sitting in the middle of the empty flatbed.

"Shit."

He returned to his cruiser and got on the radio, telling everyone they'd lost her.

His cell phone rang.

Dispatch was putting someone through who knew where Sarah was.

"Hello?"

"Yeah," a girl said, clearly out of breath, almost hysterical. "She barged in, kicked everyone out, and she had a gun, and she …"

"Slow down," Waller said. "Who are you?"

"I'm Debbie. I operate a yoga studio on Colborne on the second floor."

"Okay, take a breath. Tell me what happened."

Horns beeped behind Waller. He had flicked off the flashing lights and sat parked in front of traffic in an unmarked cruiser. He put his car in gear and pulled away.

"A girl walked into my studio, like three or four minutes ago, pulled out a gun, and ordered my students and me out the back way. We're all huddled in the alley."

"Where?"

"I just told you." She sounded exasperated. "Colborne Street, near Church Street. Yoga studio on the second floor."

"Why call me?" Waller asked as he performed a U-turn and gunned his engine.

"She said her name was Sarah Roberts. She told me to call the cops. Then she used your name."

"I'm on my way. Wait outside."

"No problem. And I got her gun."

That's mine.

"Good. Keep it."

He hung up and got on the radio, asking all units to converge on the yoga studio.

Sarah wouldn't get away again.

***

"Before you do whatever it is you've come to do," Sarah said. "Tell me why."

The ugly one stepped closer. Nausea and fear crept through her. She had the urge to shove her hand into his throat hard enough to collapse his trachea so he would die squirming like a landed fish on the floor, but she controlled her impulse to violence. Vivian knew better. Sarah had to trust the process. Things would play out without her killing anyone.

But one touch from either of these two men and she would die. Choices, choices …

"The time is upon us," Ugly said from three feet away. "End times. As the Bible has predicted. We were given the opportunity to Rapture the good ones, the people God has asked to come home. After all that you've done, Sarah, you need to go. It is your time."

"Are you Simon Peter?" she asked.

He faltered and looked at his partner. Then back at her. "How did you get my name?"

"Same way you get the information your brother Matthew gives you."

He looked genuinely stunned. "You know about Matthew, too?"

Her mind raced with possible escape plans and ways to run. Could she get seriously hurt going through the front window?

"Vivian told me."

Sarah wiped her forehead as sweat collected and rolled into her eyes. She had to keep her eyes clear to watch Simon. Simon's partner wiped his forehead, too, wetness appearing under his arms.

But Simon wasn't sweating. He didn't look hot at all. The tips of his ears were red, and his face had gained some color, but he wasn't sweating one drip. The lights in the yoga studio were bright enough to see perspiration.

"You really are something," Simon said. "But it is time to go."

"Can I have a word with God before you Rapture me?" Sarah said in a mocking tone.

Simon nodded. "Very well."

She decided to lie to delay them, waiting for Waller to bust in. They were here to send her wherever you go when you're dead because she was one of the good ones.

She so lied.

"I'd like to ask forgiveness for the man I killed unnecessarily two years ago."

"What?" the partner asked. "You killed someone?"

Sarah nodded. "May I continue?"

"Make it quick," Simon said. He turned to his partner. "And don't interrupt, Brother Philip."

"I'm sorry for all the wrongs I've committed for personal gain. For those children in the school bus I killed. Even though the man who wanted them dead had nothing to do with me, I just needed his drugs. I'm sorry for those three innocent women I murdered in their sleep so they wouldn't find out about the affair I was having with their husbands—" She stopped abruptly as Simon stumbled on his feet. "Are you okay?"

"Yes. Are you almost finished?"

The sclera of Simon's eyes had turned red, and he still wasn't sweating. His ears were dark red now, and his face had taken on even more color. Compared to Philip, Simon was as arid as a desert, whereas Philip was soaked in the one-hundred-plus heat. The sweat dripped down Sarah's back, her arms, and her neck.

"I'm sorry for all the pain and suffering I've caused over the years," she continued. Then she met Simon's eyes. "Actually, there are too many murders for me to count. Maybe we should move to the next step. I wouldn't want to delay you."

She was ready. Waller would walk in at any second now. They were mere seconds away from ending this. She was prepared to go for the groin, the neck, and the nose. Wherever she could to destabilize them. She'd been in situations like these before and walked away. Vivian couldn't be wrong. She would walk away again.

"Okay." Simon stepped forward and almost fell. He stopped, shook his head, and started toward her again.

Philip grabbed his arm and pulled him back.

"Brother Simon, we can't do this."

Simon stopped and turned to face his partner. "And why's that? It's too hot in here. We have to do this and get me outside."

"But, Simon, she has confessed to horrible things. How could God want her? The Rapture is about sending home the good ones. That's all you've been preaching. This goes against everything you've said."

"Then she's lying because she's good. But it doesn't matter. We were sent here to Rapture her. That's all we're supposed to do."

"No," Philip shouted.

Simon turned to look at him. This was Sarah's chance. She felt it and got ready to move. Then someone pounded up the stairs by the broken door.

The cavalry had arrived. She stayed where she was, with Simon and Philip between her and the door. The last thing she wanted was to get hit by a stray bullet meant for the two assholes in front of her.

"Why are you being like this?" Simon asked.

"Simon, you preached about the good ones. It is abundantly clear that Sarah Roberts isn't a good person. She has killed children. She has killed women for personal gain. We have the wrong person. There's no way I will be a part of randomly killing people."

"Then I'll have to ask you to wait outside."

"No. I will not—"

Simon moved fast. Sarah had to wipe her eyes again. When it was over, Philip had a syringe sticking out of the side of his neck. He stumbled back, away from Simon, clutching at his neck, horror in his eyes. He dropped to his knees, shook around the shoulders, and fell backward. His body was wracked with convulsions for a few seconds, and then his head lolled to the side as his body stopped shaking. He lay still in death.

Simon watched her.

"You're next," he said, holding a syringe high in the air.

"Freeze!" someone shouted behind him.

Simon was fast for all the heat and wavering on his feet. He jumped behind Sarah, crouched low, and held the needle to her neck. She had tried to smack at him but missed. She pulled away from the small pricking sensation of the needle on her neck but could only go so far.

"Step away from the door, or she dies," Simon yelled.

Parkman raised high enough over the broken door in the

corridor to take the situation in and then dropped below it.

"There's no escape. Let her go. This can only end badly for you." He popped his head up again, then stood and gingerly stepped through the broken door, a two-fisted grip on his gun. "Don't make me shoot."

Aaron stepped into the room behind Parkman, followed by his three employees.

"Hey, how did you guys get here?" Sarah asked, on the edge of passing out. At any second, she was about to be pricked by the needle and succumb to its poison. She recognized the baseball cap Alex wore. "You guys followed me."

"We couldn't let you walk into trouble," Aaron said. "I'm sorry."

Sarah's eyes watered. "You gotta stop apologizing." She met Parkman's eyes and smiled. "And you brought Parkman?"

Aaron nodded.

"This isn't the time," Simon yelled. "Step back, all of you. Get out, or Sarah dies."

"Okay," Parkman said, aiming his weapon at the ceiling. "Take it easy. All we want to do is talk."

"Then drop your weapon."

Parkman looked at Sarah. She nodded subtly with her eyes. Parkman slowly lowered his weapon to his side.

"What now?" he asked. "What do you want?"

"I want you to leave. Sarah and I were just finishing our conversation."

"That's not going to happen."

Aaron's friends fanned out along the wall, but Simon didn't appear to notice. She was pretty sure she would still walk away from this, even though a lethal needle was pressed against her neck. Vivian would've set it up right. Wouldn't she?

"You've got five seconds to get out, or I plunge this needle in her neck, and no amount of bullets will stop my thumb from depressing this plunger."

Parkman raised both hands. "Okay, okay, take it easy." He stepped back. "We'll move into the hallway. Let's talk about this. Maybe there's something you want."

Parkman continued to back up, as did Aaron. His three friends remained near the far wall. Sarah was completely drenched in sweat. Simon didn't hold her with any kind of force, just the needle tip touching her skin. She didn't want to move in case he panicked and jabbed her. She remained absolutely still as the sweat poured into her eyes. Her stomach remained unbelievably calm for what she faced. Maybe it was the buildup of violence that got people on edge. At that moment, she saw the room, felt it, and became a part of it.

Just as Parkman backed into the hallway, there was a commotion on the stairs behind him. He looked over and raised his hands in that direction.

"Hold on, Waller. I got this."

From behind the wall, Waller's deep voice said, "Step aside, Parkman, I'm coming through."

Then Waller showed his face and pulled his weapon.

"I see you've got your gun back," Sarah said.

"Game over," Waller said. "Drop the needle and step away from Sarah. There's nowhere for you to go. No escape."

Simon jammed the needle into Sarah's neck and

depressed the plunger without warning.

Sarah fell to the side and hit the floor. A gun fired. Someone screamed. Glass broke. Commotion all around. The lights flashed. Her hands went numb. Parkman shouted 'no' over and over.

Then darkness.

Chapter 30

Parkman was shocked at seeing the needle stuck in Sarah's flesh.

"No, no, no …" he shouted over and over.

Waller's gun had fired once, but the shot went wild, hitting the mirrors behind Sarah and her attacker. Parkman had recognized the man who had held Sarah from the security footage at the mall. The ugly one who suffered from ectodermal dysplasia.

He ran to Sarah, her face now peaceful. Waller walked up behind him, his gun still out.

"Look what you've done," Parkman said. Waller tried to respond, but Parkman shouted over Waller's voice. "Look what you've fucking done!"

Waller stood more than a foot over Parkman and probably weighed double, but he stepped back when he saw the look on Parkman's face.

"Everyone out," Parkman shouted. "This is a crime scene now."

Tears poured down Aaron's face. Or maybe it was sweat.

Waller hadn't put his gun away. He kept it trained on Ugly, who lay behind Sarah's body. Parkman followed Waller's gaze.

Ugly lay on his back, his body convulsing.

"What's wrong with him?" Parkman asked.

Waller shrugged.

Waller's probably afraid to speak, thought Parkman.

Ugly shook more violently as if having an epileptic seizure. His eyes rolled back in his head, and then he was still.

"Did he prick himself with that needle?"

Waller shrugged again. He lowered his weapon as Ugly was no longer a threat.

"Don't move him until the medics get here," Parkman said. "Call the coroner." He slapped Waller's arm. "This is your jurisdiction. Clean your fucking mess up."

Parkman dropped to his knees and leaned over Sarah.

"I'm so, so sorry. I failed you. It's not right that you're the victim here. It's not right."

Parkman fell to the floor and wept, tears and sweat streaming down his face.

Sarah Roberts was dead, and he would never forgive himself.

Chapter 31

The press conference came to a close. Waller walked off the little stage and away from the podium. He made his way to the back room, where his guests waited with refreshments.

He was happy with the way things had turned out. The police funerals had come and gone, successful in every way. He hadn't been an embarrassment to his colleagues as the Allandale Centre massacre was solved before the first batch of officers from around the globe arrived for the funerals.

It had been a full week since the incident in the yoga studio, and with the funerals done and the paperwork all filed, the media had just been brought up to speed on what they needed to know.

He opened the door and stepped into the cavernous room that held the people waiting to hear more of the story.

"Good afternoon, everyone. Let me get a drink for my parched throat, and I'll tell you the rest."

Heads nodded. No one said a word. They were all eager to hear the details Waller had held close for the past few days.

After pouring a large cup of coffee, Waller moved to the head of the table where he remained standing, sipped his coffee, and then set the cup down.

"As you all know, Parkman received a call from a medical specialist a couple of hours after the incident at the yoga studio." Waller paused and nodded at Parkman. "The man who had changed his name to Simon Peter was, in fact, suffering from something called ectodermal dysplasia, as Parkman had suspected. According to our sources, it affects over seven thousand people worldwide. Parkman, you want to do the honors on this part?"

Parkman pushed away from the table and stood. He adjusted his jacket and scanned the faces in the room. "Usually, there are abnormalities of two or more ectodermal structures such as teeth, digits, cranial-facial structure, hair, skin, and sweat glands. In Simon Peter's case, he had most of those abnormalities. The important one was the lack of sweat glands due to an inactive protein. This means he could not perspire. If he can't sweat, the body can't regulate its own temperature properly. Overheating becomes an issue that can lead to brain damage and even death, which is what happened in this case. Some of you who were present in the yoga studio a week ago might remember seeing Simon with the red-tipped ears and reddening face, even pinkish in color, more so than the rest of us. When Simon started having a seizure after injecting Sarah, he was in the final stages of heat stroke. We didn't know that at the time, and he was left to suffer in the one-hundred-degree temperature for another hour or more until he was removed on a stretcher, already dead."

Parkman sat down and gestured with his hand for Waller to continue.

Waller tapped the notebook on the table. "You're probably all aware by now that this was Brother Philip's notebook. Inside, we found his journal with notes on everything Simon was getting his group of Rapturites to do for him. James doubted their methods and approached Philip with his concerns, thinking that Simon would get rid of him if he were more vocal. So Philip wrote everything down in case they ever got arrested, which Philip did."

Waller took a sip of his coffee. Others around the table did the same.

"After the Allandale Centre attack, Philip had huge reservations about what they were doing, even though Simon could predict the future by supposedly talking to his dead brother, Matthew, but no one knew where Simon hid the batch of needles that were filled with pavulon, or pancuronium bromide, a muscle relaxant. It is so potent at one hundred milligrams that it completely relaxes all the muscles in the body in less than ten seconds, even the heart muscle, causing death. Simon found a way to add a little potassium chloride to the mix. What he had was basically a lethal injection found in any Texas death row prison. They use this stuff to execute prisoners."

He drank more coffee and then continued. "According to Philip, once Simon showed him the storage unit in the basement of their apartment building, Philip had a way to stop him. They ran when they were worried we would come and arrest them after what happened to Thomas. Philip was ordered to grab the needles from the storage unit. He did, but he had filled them with saline solution the previous evening, replacing the lethal chemicals." Waller nodded at his esteemed guest, who sat beside Aaron and his three instructors from the dojo. "That's what saved your life, Sarah."

Sarah Roberts brushed a strand of hair out of her face and leaned forward. "My hands went numb after the injection. I think Vivian shut me down to control the scene better. But you and I still have a problem to solve, Waller."

He nodded. "You're right, we do. The Americans fed us a bunch of shit about you being the target." He looked down at the notebook. "This documented proof of their plan to kill you, oh, excuse me, Rapture you, absolved you of any wrongdoing. In the end, you were the victim here. The Americans were after you, the bad guys were after you, and I was, too. I'm sorry, Sarah Roberts, for my part in that."

"I'm getting used to it. Only Parkman has ever known that I'm the innocent one." She winked at him. He tapped her hand.

"What I still don't get," Waller said, "was how you knew to lead Simon to the hot yoga studio. That was brilliant. Then you stalled him long enough with your lies of the sins you've committed. By doing that, you were killing him. How did you know?"

"I didn't know. Vivian told me to not shoot them. She also told me to lead them to the yoga studio. I trust her. I don't always need to know everything. I leave that up to my sister."

"Your dead sister?" Waller asked.

"Yup."

"I have a hard time believing that since there's nothing out there beyond this life," Waller said, waving an arm in the air.

"You don't have to believe it. It's only important that I do."

He stared at her a moment longer, the room silent. "I guess you're right."

She smiled for a second, then her lips dropped into a flat line. Waller looked away.

"That about sums it up," he said. "We have Philip and Thomas in custody. They're both charged with multiple counts of first-degree murder. A lot of planning went into snatching Rod Howley, killing Hank's wife, Drake Bellamy, and then Sarah's friends south of the border. I'm sorry for that, too, Sarah. It sounds like it's been a long, tough few weeks for you."

"Yeah, I just want to go home."

"That's been arranged. We have a car waiting for you and Parkman to take you to the airport. You fly out in a few hours."

Sarah stood and walked out of the room, Aaron on her heels. Waller stayed behind to talk to his superiors as Parkman still wanted to know where Waller had planned on taking Sarah that night he picked her up at the hotel on Yonge Street. Waller was prepared to tell the truth.

But first, he pulled his badge out and placed it on the table beside his gun.

"I'm resigning."

Waller went to his office to empty his desk. He left his coffee on the conference room table.

He knew Parkman would be happy, but he didn't care. He couldn't remain on the force after what he had planned to do to Sarah.

The innocent Sarah Roberts.

Once he had his desk cleaned out, he would direct investigators to the secluded farmhouse with the basement where he planned on taking Sarah that night. The basement with the cage and chains where he would victimize her for a few weeks for what she had done to his platoon. His men would have been proud. Officers protect their own.

Now that he had learned the truth, it would have been the wrong thing to do.

He was an embarrassment.

Waller walked to his desk, head down, Parkman on his heels.

Chapter 32

Sarah Roberts fired up her BMW F800R, put on her helmet and backpack, straddled the bike, and set off.

With her parents' blessing, it was time for Sarah to hit the road and see her country as it was meant to be. She had traveled to Europe and spent over a month in the Toronto area but had never toured America. It was the first time in a long time that no one had hunted her. She had no outstanding arrest warrants, and the Sophia Project had died with Hank's and Rod's deaths.

She was free.

Aaron had been the biggest hurdle, wanting her to stay with him in Toronto. But Sarah couldn't. She missed Drake, and then she had the Rapturites after her. There were too many memories. Too many bad ones.

She needed to break free, move on.

Parkman understood. He had accompanied her back to the States, visited her parents with her, and then headed back to work. He put in for a transfer as soon as he clocked back in. Santa Rosa, California, was his destination, or somewhere in that area. Sarah's parents were moving. They wanted to live closer to the coast in wine country, and Parkman wanted to stay close to them if anything cropped up later in Sarah's life when he would be needed.

Caleb and Amelia, Sarah's parents, had thought it a lovely gesture and welcomed Parkman as more than a family friend. They offered their new home to him anytime he needed it, as he was a member of the Roberts family now.

It pleased Sarah to see her parents warm up to the only real friend she'd ever had.

She had stayed in her old bedroom for a few weeks until the move to Santa Rosa. The house sold, and the new one was smaller, allowing her parents to pay it off completely with the chunk of cash left over.

They bought Sarah the new motorcycle after putting enough money in a bank account for her to travel for a couple of years.

The California sun was dropping as Sarah set off. Her first stop was somewhere in Las Vegas, Nevada. Vivian had asked her to do a few small tasks that would have large ramifications if left unfulfilled.

Sarah had packed a Mac Book Pro to start writing a memoir of what happened to her over the last few years. She decided to start with the kidnapping over four years ago when her dark visions began.

"That's what I'll call it," she said to herself. "Dark Visions."

In her breast pocket were a notepad and two pens. Even though she appeared to ride alone, Sarah had a companion. Vivian rode with her toward another chapter in Sarah's life.

Sarah would alter the course of events within thirty-six hours, and her life would change forever.

She was no longer *The Victim*.

Sarah became *The Enigma*.

About Jonas Saul

Jonas Saul is the bestselling author of the Sarah Roberts
Series—more than two million sold!—and has written
and published over sixty thrillers. After acquiring an
agent, he signed several deals in Los Angeles, with
MadRiver Pictures optioning his Sarah Roberts Series—
over forty books!—(currently in development).

Jonas has often outranked Stephen King and Dean

Koontz on Amazon over the past decade. He's regularly invited to be a guest speaker, teacher, or workshop presenter at international writing conferences and film festivals worldwide. He hosts an annual writer's retreat in Greece, where he currently lives. He focuses his teaching on how to get tension and emotion in every scene, on every page, how he made it as a creator/writer, the path to success in this business, and the pitfalls to avoid. He also hosts a reading retreat in Greece with guest authors, yoga retreats, and hiking retreats. Visit the Imagine Greece Retreats website at www.imaginegreeceretreats.com, or email him directly to discuss an opportunity to join one of the retreats at jonas@imaginegreeceretreats.com.

Jonas is also a professional freelance editor. He works for several publishers and does private editing for clients, with many testimonials on his website at www.imaginepress.org, which details each author's response to Jonas's editing skills. Email Jonas directly for an editing quote at editor@imaginepress.org.

To book Jonas for a speaking engagement at a writer's conference/festival, to have him on your jury at a film festival, or even to say hello, email Jonas directly at jonassaul@icloud.com.

For updates on releases, hit the "Follow" button on Amazon or Bookbub, and join Jonas on Facebook, where he's most active.

Contact Jonas Saul

Linktree: Find me here

Email: jonassaul@icloud.com